"Chuck would be good for you."

Shad's voice was hard as he continued, "You really should marry him, Charley."

Tears stung Charley's eyes—tears of anger and frustration., "Why is everyone pushing me at Chuck? No one has even bothered to ask me what *I* want!"

"I know what you want." Shad's gaze centered on her lips, and the desire that burned in his eyes stole her anger. His mouth began a slow descent toward hers, stopping before their lips touched. His breath caressed her, his smell intoxicated her, and she felt dizzy as he murmured, "I'm no good for you, Charley. But it doesn't seem to matter, does it?"

"No," she whispered, and stopped listening to her common sense.

JANET DAILEY AMERICANA

THE TRAVELLING KIND

Harlequin Books

TORONTO • NEW YORK • LONDON
AMSTERDAM • PARIS • SYDNEY • HAMBURG
STOCKHOLM • ATHENS • TOKYO • MILAN

The state flower depicted on the cover of this book is
syringa.

Janet Dailey Americana edition published November 1986
ISBN 373-21912-1

Harlequin Presents edition published May 1981
Second printing May 1988

Original hardcover edition published in 1981
by Mills & Boon Limited

CHAPTER ONE

THE SUN-WARMED AIR blowing in through the opened windows of the pickup truck was fragrant with the resiny scent of pines. Charley Collins was too preoccupied with her thoughts to notice the pine fragrance of the breeze in more than a passing way. It showed in the long, unsmiling set of her mouth, lips pressed together in a concentrating line. A tiny crease in her forehead marred the smooth suntanned features, and the hazel green of her eyes was clouded with many thoughts.

Her attention was abstractly centered on the highway she traveled, her gaze rarely lifting from the concrete road to the Idaho mountains. She drove the truck with a competence born of long experience, an experience that came from learning to drive almost before her legs were long enough to reach the floor pedals. It had been the same with horses, learning to ride before her feet reached the stirrups.

The winding stretch of forest-flanked road was broken by the appearance of a building that housed a combination service station-café-general store with living quarters in the rear. Charley slowed the truck as she approached her destination. Swinging off the highway, the pickup rolled past the gasoline pumps to stop in front of the wooden building.

With the gear shifted to park, Charley switched off the ignition key and opened the door. The riding heel of her western boot dug into the gravel as she stepped from the cab. The faded blue denim of her snug-fitting Levi's had been worn soft, a comfortable second skin stretched over her slim hips and long legs. The long sleeves of her plaid blouse were rolled up, revealing tanned forearms, and the pearl snaps of the Western blouse were unfastened at the throat to hint at more suntanned skin.

There was a supple grace in the looseness of her stride as she walked to the entrance door of the station office-café-store. A tortoiseshell clasp held her thick, sandy hair together at the back of her neck, its heavy length swaying as she walked.

The bell above the door jingled to announce her entrance into the building. She was greeted by the tantalizing aroma of homemade doughnuts and freshly brewed coffee from the café section, marked by a horseshoe-shaped counter. As she paused to close the door her glance touched the outfit propped against the wall. It consisted of a rolled duffel bag, an A-fork saddle that was well made and showed use, and a wool saddle pad and blanket along with an assortment of other gear that bore the earmarks of quality. The tools of his trade said a lot about a cowboy. Normally Charley's curiosity would have prompted her to study his outfit, but she had other things on her mind.

Her searching glance briefly noted the cowboy slouching indolently at the counter on a high stool. Since he was the only customer, he was also the likely owner of the outfit by the door. A noise from the kitchen drew her attention and a smile widened her mouth as a stocky man in a bibbed white apron appeared.

"Hello, Frank." Long graceful strides ate up the short distance to the counter to greet the owner. "How've you been?"

"As I live and breathe! Charley Collins!" He

came forward to glad-hand her, his lined face wreathing into a smile, a salting of gray in his brown hair. "I haven't seen hide nor hair of you since spring."

"I've been keeping busy." Which was an understatement.

His expression immediately became regretful. "How's Gary? We were all sorry to hear about the accident." Then he motioned toward the stool she was standing beside. "Sit down. I'll pour you a cup of coffee on the house."

"No, thank you, but—" She tried to protest but he'd already set a cup on the counter and was filling it from the glass pot. She sat one hip on the stool, keeping a foot on the floor while the other rested on the footrail around the counter. "Gary is doing much better, although he's fit to be tied."

"I can imagine." Frank Doyle laughed, the laughter fading into a compassionate smile. "With Gary not able to get around, it really must put a heavy burden on you."

"Actually that's why I'm here." Charley took the opening she'd been given. "Gary is going to be in that cast for another six weeks. I was hoping I could hire Lonnie to help me out on the ranch for the rest of the summer." Lonnie Doyle was Frank's teenage son. He'd worked part-time for them before when they'd needed an extra hand. Charley knew he was a good worker and dependable.

"Sorry. Lonnie has a full-time job as a laborer on a road crew this summer. I know he'd help you out on the weekends if it would help."

Charley blew out a tired sigh and slanted her lips into a smiling grimace. "We need someone every day. Between taking care of Gary and the ranch work, I have my hands full. It's more than I can handle alone," she admitted. "But I may have to settle for someone part-time. So far, everyone I've asked already has a job."

"What about Andy Hollister?" Frank suggested.

"He's drinking again. I can't depend on him." The shake of her head decisively dismissed that possibility.

As she started to lift the steaming mug of black coffee to her mouth a third voice intruded on the conversation with a soft, interested drawl.

"Excuse me, Miss, but did I hear you say you're looking for someone to do ranch work?"

Charley angled her chin in the direction of the cowboy seated at the top of the horseshoe counter and lifted her gaze to inspect him. A sweat-stained, brown Stetson was pushed to the back of his head, revealing heavy black hair. Long hours in the sun had burned layers of tan into the skin stretched across the angular planes of his face. Its teak color combined with crow-black hair to contrast with the glittering blue eyes that returned her study. He was sitting loosely, all muscles relaxed. His large-knuckled hands were folded around the coffee cup, nursing it, his browned fingers showing the roughness of callouses. A smiling knowledge lurked around him, a touch of irony that said he wasn't easily fooled. In his mid-thirties, he was a prime specimen of manhood, handsome in the craggy way of a man of the West.

It was impossible to judge his height, but she could guess at the corded muscles beneath the faded blue-and-gold plaid of his shirt. There was another quality about him that Charley recognized—the restless streak of a drifter. She had seen it before and experienced a twinge of regret that it should be a trait of his.

When her keen assessment of him was finished, she responded to his inquiry. "Yes, we are looking for help at the ranch."

"I could use the job," he stated in that same lazy drawl of interest. His slow indifference was deceptive, his gaze alive to her, sweeping over her with a returning assessment.

Charley felt the earthy sensuality that was within his look; nothing offensive, just an honest male admiration for a member of the opposite sex. It created a vague disturbance warning Charley of her susceptibility.

Her glance darted to the outfit propped against the wall near the door, aware that it spoke for his competence. This stranger was her first applicant for the job. Although she would have preferred hiring someone locally, the situation was too desperate. She couldn't afford to be too choosy.

But common sense insisted that she make an inquiry about his experience. "Where have you worked before?"

"I worked for Cord Harris on the Circle H in Texas, Kincaid's spread in Oklahoma. Most recently for the Triple C in Montana."

"We have a small two-man operation, nothing close to the size of the ranches you've mentioned," Charley explained, impressed by the list. "There's a lot of work that will have to be done afoot." And there were some hard-line cowboys who turned up their nose at any task that couldn't be done on horseback.

He glanced down at his large work-roughened

hands, then lifted his gaze, sharply blue and glinting. "I've done physical labor before... and survived."

"We can't pay much," Charley warned. "You'd get a salary, plus room and board." She named a sum she and Gary had agreed upon.

"Sounds fair to me." He shrugged his acceptance and uncurled his hands from around the coffee cup, flattening them on the counter. He used them to push off the stool, dismounting almost as if it was a horse. Reaching into his pocket he pulled out some change and laid it on the counter to pay for his coffee, then moved around the corner to Charley, extending a hand. "The name is Shad Russell."

"Mr. Russell." She acknowledged the introduction as her hand was engulfed in the hugeness of his. Again she felt that vague disturbance flutter along her nerve ends, warning her to be careful around him.

He was taller than she had expected, easily six foot. Charley slid off the stool to negate some of the difference in their height. There was a lean and hungry look about him as he stood before her with loose-limbed ease. He was a man with a big appetite for many things—excitement, life, women and adventure. She watched rolled on him before Gary could kick free. He ended up with a compound fracture of the upper leg bone. He is in a cast up to his hip...and will be for another six weeks.''

"That's rough.''

That was an understatement in Charley's opinion. It pulled a sighing laugh from her throat. "He isn't adjusting to the restrictions of a broken leg too well. He lumbers around the house like a bear with its paw in a trap, growling and snapping at everything, so be prepared. He acts more like a rebellious teenager than a man of thirty.''

"How old are you?''

She turned to find him studying her through heavy-lidded eyes, so blue and sharp with male interest. She fought down the sudden acceleration of her pulse. "Twenty-six. Why?'' She managed a smooth response and countered with a question.

"Divorced?''

She wanted to tell him that his questions were becoming too personal, but on second thought she decided against it. A certain frankness seemed to be in order so a relationship could be established and maintained for the rest of the summer...if Shad Russell stayed that long.

"Never been married," she admitted to her single status, using an indifferent tone.

"No fiancé in the wings, either?" His sidelong glance was taking in the maturity of her figure and the cleanness of her profile.

"None." Her reply was cheerful, if a little defiant.

"For a woman of twenty-six, that usually means she was jilted somewhere down the line and hasn't recovered from a broken heart," Shad observed. "Especially when you're talking about an attractive woman like you."

The last comment was designed to have an effect on her and it did, but Charley didn't let it show, except to laugh it off. "Sorry. There is nothing so melodramatic in my past."

"Then how have you managed to stay single?" His curiosity was aroused. She could hear it in the inflection of his voice.

"Actually it was easy." She cast him a bland glance. "Around here, if you don't marry your high-school steady or go on to college to check out that marriage market, you don't find much husband material. The men are either already married or too young or too old—or like you."

"Like me?" Her remark caused him to lift a dark eyebrow and give her a penetrating look that was both curious and amused.

"Yes. You are the traveling kind—just passing through on your way to some other place, never content to stay anywhere too long." She had recognized his type right from the beginning, which didn't lessen his attraction. Men who were rogues always held a fatal fascination for women. She wasn't an exception, but at least she knew the danger signals.

"Is that a bad way to live?" Shad Russell sounded amused, mocking almost.

"Not for you, maybe," Charley conceded. "But it can be bad for the girl who is foolish enough to think she can change you."

"And you aren't a fool." It came out soft, a borderline challenge.

"No, I'm not a fool." She smiled without humor and continued to look at the road ahead. She was nearing the turnoff to the ranch and slowed the truck to edge off the pavement onto the dirt lane. "This is Seven Bar land. The ranch house sits a couple of miles back from the highway."

Although he didn't change his relaxed position, Charley was conscious that he became more alert to his surroundings, the sharpness of his gaze taking mental notes on the abundance of graze, the condition of the cattle and fences— things a cowboy needed to know to do his job.

17

She didn't question his ability. The one flaw Charley could see in his character was that broad streak of wanderlust. It would never do to rely on him too much. The thought saddened her, but she didn't examine too closely the reason why it depressed her.

The mountain lane wound along the slope and opened into a meadow where the ranch headquarters was situated with a panoramic vista of the surrounding peaks. Besides the two-story white wood house, there was a log barn and shed and a set of corrals of rough-cut timber. It was a small operation by modern standards but its clean, well-kept appearance was a source of pride for Charley. A half-used stack of last summer's hay stood near the barn, with the summer's yet to be cut. The horses in the corral whickered a greeting and rushed to the front rail as she slowed the pickup to a stop in front of the house.

"Our facilities don't stretch to include a bunkhouse," she explained to Shad Russell. "There is a spare bedroom in the house you can use."

A mongrel cow dog trotted out from the shade of the house to greet her. The sight of the stranger climbing out of the cab of the truck changed the dog's pace to a stiff-legged walk.

The mongrel sniffed suspiciously at his legs but a low word from Shad started its tail wagging and a panting grin opened its mouth. Charley observed the dog's acceptance of the new hired hand without comment and waited at the porch steps for him to join her.

Leaving the saddle in the back of the truck for the time being, Shad lifted out his duffel bag and started toward the house. There was no hurry in his long stride as his gaze made a slow study of the ranch and its buildings. When his eyes stopped on her they held the glint of approval. The curve of her mouth softened under its light.

"It looks like you and your brother have a sound, well-run operation here," he observed.

False modesty didn't come naturally to her so she admitted, "We like to think so." She turned to climb the steps. "Come in and meet my brother and I'll show you where to put your things."

He followed her up the steps and across the porch floor, his footsteps an echo of her own. She pulled open the screen door and entered the front room with Shad behind her. The loud thumping of crutches sounded from the solitary downstairs bedroom.

"Is that you, Charley?" Her brother's voice

called impatiently as the steady thud of the crutches moved closer to the front room. She opened her mouth to make an affirmative answer but he spoke again before she had a chance. "Damn it all! Where have you been all this time? You said you'd only be gone a couple of hours!"

"It took longer than I thought," Charley replied and would have said more but her brother appeared in the archway of the hall leading off the front room. When she saw him she didn't know whether to be embarrassed or laugh at his predicament. A bulky plaster cast encased the whole of his right leg. His chambray shirt was half buttoned, the tails hanging free but not concealing the jockey shorts he was wearing. A pair of jeans was trapped in a hand gripping the crutch of his left side. Her brother stopped short at the sight of the stranger beside Charley, a dull red creeping up his neck.

"Meet our new hired hand, Gary." She just barely managed to contain the smile that was playing with the corners of her mouth. "This is Shad Russell. And the half-naked man with the broken leg is my brother, Gary Collins." As she half-turned toward Shad Russell she caught the glint of humor that was quickly veiled.

There wasn't any way for her brother to

gracefully get out of his embarrassing situation so he chose to ignore it. "Russell," he repeated the name in a searching way. "Are you from around here?" he frowned at his inability to place the name.

"No," Shad replied and volunteered no more information than that.

"Why don't you follow me, Shad?" Charley suggested, moving toward the staircase. "I'll show you where you'll be bunking."

"Good idea." His lazy blue gaze slid from her brother to her, aware that she was rescuing her brother from an awkward situation.

The door to the stairwell stood open. Charley preceded him up the steps and paused in the hallway of the second floor. When he stood beside her, there didn't seem to be as much room as she remembered. It took her a second to realize that she was feeling the effect of his nearness, the breadth of his shoulders and the towering leanness of his height. She opened the door fronting the staircase.

"This is the bathroom." She unnecessarily identified the room, then pointed to the door below the washbasin. "The towels and washcloths are kept in there." She saw his gaze light on the bottles of makeup and lotions on the surrounding counter and didn't bother to mention that they would be sharing the facility. "You'll have the bedroom to the right of the stairs." He backed out of the bathroom doorway and let her take the lead.

When Charley entered his assigned room, she found herself avoiding the area where the double bed stood. She walked instead to the closet. "There are extra blankets on the top shelf if you need them. There are some wire hangers in the closet for your clothes. Let me know if you need more."

When she turned, she realized he hadn't been paying much attention to her. His gaze was skimming the contents of the room, skipping the furniture to inspect the pictures on the wall and the assorted knickknacks on the bedside table and dresser. None of them were special or out of the ordinary. Charley was confused by his absorption in them. When the silence ran on, his gaze shifted back to her. His mouth twisted in a self-mocking smile.

"It's been years since I've slept in an actual bedroom," he explained. "I'd forgotten some of the little things that make it different."

Her glance ran around the homey room, suddenly seeing it through the eyes of someone who had spent most of his time in bunkhouses. The personal touches did stand out. She began con-

22

sidering the loneliness of his existence, then realized sharply that she was treading on dangerous ground. His life-style was one he had chosen. He had the ability to change it—*if* that was what he wanted to do, which it obviously wasn't.

"I'll leave you to unpack and settle in," she said briskly, moving toward the door. "Come down whenever you're finished."

Without waiting for a reply she left the room and ran lightly down the steps in search of her brother. She found him, still half dressed, rummaging through her sewing basket, balanced unsteadily on his crutches.

"Gary, what on earth are you looking for?" she asked with a hint of exasperation. He'd become almost childlike.

"I'm trying to find the damned scissors," he grumbled.

"Scissors?"

"Yes, scissors," he snapped irritably. "So I can cut the pant leg off these jeans. I can't get them over the cast and I'm tired of running around in a bathrobe. I want some clothes on for a change."

"If you asked me nicely, I might do it for you," Charley suggested.

He glowered at her over his shoulder. She

stood with her arms crossed in front of her in silent challenge. His hair was a darker shade of brown than her own light color but he had the same hazel eyes. His build was heavier and carried more muscle than her slender frame, but a stranger would instantly guess they were brother and sister. Their resemblance was strong in other ways, too. Both possessed the same proud, stubborn streak that often produced a contest of wills, as now. This time it was Gary who surrendered.

He sighed tiredly. "Would you cut my pants for me, please?"

"Of course." Her smile was wide and filled with warmth as she reached out to take the jeans from him. "The scissors are in the bureau drawer, not the basket."

Gary leaned on his crutches and watched her snipping at the leg of his jeans. "How come you hired this stranger? I thought we agreed to get one of the local boys." It was a statement, not an opening for an argument.

"They're all working. When I stopped in at Frank's to see if his son was available, this Shad Russell was there and asked for the job," she explained how it had come about.

"Where is he from?" he frowned curiously.

"Here and there. I didn't ask specifically," Charley admitted.

"What kind of experience does he have?"

"His list of previous employers reads like the *Who's Who* of the cattle business," she replied dryly as the scissors sliced through the last bit of cloth. "Sit down in that chair and we'll see if we can get your pants on."

Gary maneuvered awkwardly to sit on the edge of a straight chair, resting his crutches against the side. With the cast holding his leg stiff, it was a struggle working the jeans to where he could get both feet through the pant legs. When he could finally stand up again, Charley pulled the Levi's the rest of the way up.

"What you're saying is this guy is a drifter." Gary continued on with the subject as he succeeded in balancing himself on the crutches long enough to fasten his pants.

"That's right." She returned the scissors to their place in the bureau drawer. "I didn't think it mattered since we wouldn't want him to stay past summer anyway."

"No, it doesn't I guess," he agreed. "What are you going to fix for lunch?"

Charley glanced at the clock. It was an hour before noon. "All you think about anymore is your stomach," she chided him. "As much as you've been eating lately, you're going to gain twenty pounds before you get that cast off.''

"You try dragging this deadweight around with you—'' he gestured toward the cast ''—and you'll work up an appetite, too,'' he retorted.

"During these next six weeks that you're convalescing, why don't you learn to cook?'' Charley suggested. "That will be one less chore for me to do.''

The sibling discussion was interrupted by footsteps on the stairs. Charley turned as Shad Russell emerged from the stairwell. His blue glance rested briefly on her, then shifted to her brother. Yet, in that second, all her senses were brought to full awareness.

"I thought I'd take my saddle and tack to the barn, then have a look around,'' Shad stated his intentions.

"I'll come with you and give you a rundown on our operation,'' Gary volunteered, adjusting the crutches under his arms to hobble with the man. "Charley can get lunch ready while we're gone.''

A few minutes past noon, they sat down at the kitchen table to eat the lunch Charley had fixed. During the meal the conversation centered on ranch topics that ranged from work needing to be done to the cattle market and futures. Charley could tell her brother was impressed by the indifferent flow of knowledge that came from Shad Russell. His experience in the business was wide and far-reaching, yet it was revealed in a manner that could only be described as offhand. He had a keen and intelligent mind, able to discard ranching methods that didn't suit their operation and discuss others that could be incorporated to improve their present system. There never was a critical comment from Shad, nor any attempt to force a suggestion on them. An idea was idly mentioned, discussed and judged on its own merits to be either considered or rejected by Gary.

Shad Russell was becoming more and more of an enigma to Charley. He had traits she could admire in a man—his intelligence, his tact, and his quiet authority—but she never permitted herself to lose sight of the fact that he was a drifter. Today he was here, but he might be gone on the morrow.

Dessert was a fudge cake that Charley had baked the day before, and strong black coffee. When it was consumed, Shad leaned back in his chair, stretching with the contentment of a man whose stomach is full. His dancing blue gaze swung to Charley and she watched again as a smile broke from the corners of his

27

eyes, slashing lines in his lean bronze cheeks.

"It's been so long since I've sat down to a home-cooked meal, I had forgotten how good it can taste."

It was a sincere compliment with no attempt at flattery. Reaching out to her, it stroked her senses like a caress.

All she could think of was that old adage: the way to a man's heart is through his stomach.... Shaken by the thought, for she knew it wasn't possible to permanently tame a wild thing—it would always revert to its old ways—she warned herself again not to become involved with a man who was only passing through her life.

So she took his compliment and responded to it with a casual reply. "My mother was an excellent cook. I was taught by the best." She rose to clear the table of dishes and paused to offer, "More coffee?"

"No, thanks," Shad refused with the same lazy smile in place. "I thought I'd spend the afternoon riding around to familiarize myself with the layout of the ranch. Is it all right if I take my pick of the horses?"

"Ride whatever one you want." Gary gave him complete freedom in his selection.

When his departing footsteps became echoes in her mind, Charley paused in her stacking of the dirty dishes to glance at her silent brother. He was staring thoughtfully into space. A shooting twinge of pain broke his reverie and he grimaced, his hand reaching down to grip the hard cast encasing his thigh.

"Have you taken any of those pain pills the doctor prescribed for you?" Charley eyed him in silent accusation, already guessing the answer.

"No," he admitted defensively. "I don't want to start depending on pills."

"You want to be the big strong hero gritting his teeth in the face of pain," she chided him.

Gary changed the subject. "That Shad is a walking encyclopedia about ranching. I feel as if I've just spent an hour in school over lunch. That guy is sharp."

"Yes." Charley turned back to her dishes, uncomfortable with the subject he'd introduced.

"In a way, it's a rotten shame he's using all that talent working for someone else," he remarked. "But I can't help feeling we were lucky that you stumbled onto him. The man knows his business, I have no doubt about that. What do you suppose makes a man with so much going for him turn into a wandering fool?"

"I really don't know." But she wished she did.

Her gaze lifted to the window above the sink with its view of the barns and adjoining corrals. She saw Shad riding away and recognized the horse instantly. Dollar was a solid bay gelding without any markings except for a circle of white on his forehead the size of a silver dollar. He was the best all-around horse in the string, which showed that Shad Russell was a good judge of horseflesh.

CHAPTER TWO

THE ALARM CLOCK went off precisely at five o'clock the next morning. Charley rolled over with a groan while her hand fumbled over the nightstand to find the clock and shut it off. The urge was strong to go back to sleep and ignore the strident summons but her conscience wouldn't let her. She tried to push the sleep from her face without success and lethargically swung her legs from beneath the bedcovers onto the floor.

Her eyes were heavy with sleep, opened to mere slits as she stumbled to the chair where her cotton bathrobe was lying. She slipped into it out of habit rather than conscious direction and made for the door. Outside her room, the second floor was quiet—nothing and no one stirring. Not fully awake, yet not sleepwalking, either, Charley drifted down the stairs in a hazy consciousness that fell somewhere in between the two extremes.

By instinct she was guided to the kitchen. Her mind had memorized how to make coffee until she could literally do it with her eyes closed. When the percolator was plugged into the wall socket, she leaned back against the counter and let her head rest against the upper cupboard. Propped in a standing position, she let herself sink into a half sleep until the aroma of freshly perked coffee would stir her. But it was a man's voice that roused her first.

"Good morning."

Her lashes flickered long enough to give her a glimpse of the tall, lean man with crow-black hair and clear blue eyes as he came into the kitchen. She was too sleepy to be disturbed from her relaxed position.

"Is it? I haven't been able to wake up long enough to find out if it's a good morning or not," Charley murmured with her eyes closed.

There was a pulsebeat of silence before the low drawling voice came back. "You need to be kissed awake."

For some reason the comment struck Charley as being pleasantly amusing and she slanted her lips into a faint smile. Then a pair of hands were on her waist, pulling her away from the support of the kitchen cupboards. Startled by the unexpected contact, her eyes flashed open to witness the roguish glint of a blue pair regarding her so steadily. Her hands came up to ward him off but when they came in contact with the muscled flatness of his chest, they lost their purpose. Surprise had tipped her head back, bringing it into line with the one bending toward her. Its movement slid her glance to the malely drawn mouth, hypnotizing her with its steady approach.

When the warm possession of his mouth claimed her lips, she savored the heady glow of pleasure that swamped her senses. Her pliant body allowed itself to be enfolded by the circling pair of arms and yielded to the dominating outline of his hard, male length. The drugging fire of his kiss spread through her veins and ignited a response that had her kissing him back. She was more than content in his embrace, filled with a sense of rightness that had no basis in reality.

A coolness swept over her lips when he removed his mouth to end the kiss. More coolness was interjected between them as he allowed a space to be created. A little dazed, she blinked her round hazel eyes at him. She had been kissed by a stranger—a hired hand at that. She was confused about why she had permitted it to happen and why he had done it.

He turned away from her, reaching for a coffee cup to be filled from the freshly brewed pot. "You're fully awake now," he observed.

"Yes." Awake to the needs of her body and awake to him—the sharply cut profile of polished teak, the sure touch of his hands and the lime fragrance of his after-shave. But most of all she was awakened by the searing influence of his kiss.

"Would you like me to pour you a cup?" His sidelong glance was alive with knowledge of his effect on her.

"Yes," she repeated the affirmative, finally stirring from her position at the counter. "Why did you kiss me just now?" she frowned in wary demand.

"Sheer impulse."

He turned to offer her the cup in his hand, that roguish male vitality glittering in his eyes as he held her gaze. He was still standing very close to her, fully dressed, so much more in command of himself and the situation than she was. "When I walked into the kitchen, it was such a domestic scene—the little woman in her housecoat and her caramel-colored hair all disheveled from sleep, waiting for her man to come downstairs for that first cup of coffee.''

The reference to her appearance was accompanied by a skimming glance that prompted Charley to pull the cotton robe more tightly closed in front and comb her fingers through the heavy tangle of her hair in an attempt to bring it to some kind of order. The mocking glint of laughter in his look brought a trace of pink to her cheeks. Charley wasn't sure whether the rush of heat came from anger of embarrassment—or the intimacy implied in his use of the words "little woman" and "her man."

"A morning kiss seemed to be in order," Shad finished his explanation and moved with a gliding stride to the table. Pulling out a chair, he sat down and let his gaze return to her. "I've never been one to observe the rules of proper conduct. I'd be lying if I apologized for my behavior. I can't imagine being sorry for kissing a beautiful woman, even if she happens to be the boss's sister."

She was trembling with the force of the confused upheaval taking place within. She had found too much pleasure in his kiss to want him to regret it had taken place. It would be foolish and childish to make an issue out of something

35

so harmless. She simply wasn't the type to play the outraged female; besides, she had responded to him and he knew it. Yet it wasn't a course of action that she wanted to pursue, so perhaps she should straighten that point out right now.

"Mr. Russell—" she began in a crisp, authoritative tone.

But he interrupted. "Shad," he corrected with a mischievous glint in his eye.

"Very well, Shad." She conceded that formality at this point was a little ludicrous. "I think we should get our positions clear. In a couple of months or less, you are going to be moving on—to another job, maybe to another state. Your kind always think there is greener grass somewhere else. I won't deny that you are a good-looking man, but while you're here, you can practice your charms on someone else.

"I don't want to become involved with you, Shad. You are only interested in a casual flirtation or a brief affair. You don't want any relationship that will tie you down. I've had my share of meaningless relationships. Now I'm looking for something that is solid and lasting, so don't expect me to be any more than friendly toward you from now on. You'll have to find someone else to provide your female entertainment."

Her statement had turned out to be more of a speech. When she finished, his expression had become sober and withdrawn, his gaze never leaving her. He lifted his cup in a toasting acknowledgment, his mouth twisting into a rueful line.

"The message is received and understood," he said, letting his gaze fall to the black depths of the liquid in his cup. "I don't think you could have made it any plainer, Charley." Then a reckless smile edged the corners of his mouth. "Maybe that's the key. If I keep calling you Charley long enough, I'll start forgetting about the body that goes with the name." He looked up in time to see the flush of heat warm her face. His glance lingered for a stimulating second on the jutting swell of her breasts beneath the thin cotton robe. "Sorry if it embarrasses you, Charley, but you don't have a brick out of place."

"It doesn't embarrass me," she insisted, but his observation was unnerving. She wasn't sure that she wanted him to find her physically attractive. There was too much potential for danger in that. At the same moment, she realized that she was asking for trouble by staying in the same room with him when she was wearing only a nightgown and robe. She set the untouched cup of coffee on the counter. "Excuse me. It's time I was dressed."

"I couldn't agree with you more," Shad murmured against the rim of his coffee cup, thus hiding the smile Charley suspected was lurking at the corners of his mouth.

Twenty minutes later she came downstairs dressed in her work clothes for the day, worn Levi's and a rust-colored blouse with its long tails knotted at the front waistband. The aroma of bacon permeated the air and Charley faltered in mid stride, then continued toward the kitchen where the smell was stronger.

Shad was standing at the stove when she walked in. He glanced at her over his shoulder. "How do you like your eggs? Scrambled? Over easy?"

"Over easy," she responded without thinking, the frown of surprised disbelief not leaving her face. "You didn't have to fix your own breakfast. I was coming down to do it," she insisted defensively.

"Some women take longer than others to dress. I wasn't sure which category you belonged in." Shad spoke with the certainty of experience. "I wanted to get an early start today so I decided against waiting for you. Do you ob-

ject to someone else cooking in your kitchen?"
he asked as an afterthought.

"No," she replied with a shake of her tawny
hair, watching him deftly flip an egg in the hot
bacon grease of the skillet without damaging the
yolk. It was obvious he was no stranger to a
kitchen.

"Is something wrong?"

"No. I guess I'm just amazed that you know
how to cook. Most men don't bother to learn—
my brother, for instance. Why did you?" There
seemed to be any number of things about this
man that separated him from the crowd.

"It was a case of necessity," he replied with
an indifferent lift of his shoulder as he scooped
the fried egg out of the grease with a metal
turner, then slid it onto the plate warming
on the stove. Using a pair of tongs, he added a
rasher of bacon and handed the plate to Charley. "The way I live, I have to be self-reliant.
There is toast on the table."

The table had been set for two and Charley
sat down in front of one of the place settings to
eat this breakfast prepared by someone else. It
was a novel experience, a definitely pleasant
change of pace. She was spreading dewberry
jam on her toast when Shad joined her at the
table. Her glance ran over this apparently multi-

talented man. Strength and raw vitality were a part of his smoothly hewn features, a smiling knowledge of life always lurking in his eyes. He had aroused her interest in him as a man, and also her curiosity about him as a person.

"Where are you from originally, Shad?" She wondered about his background and what had prompted his restless life-style—never staying anywhere too long, always passing through to some other place.

"I was raised mostly in Colorado." He cut into his fried egg, not showing any reluctance to talk about his past.

"Do you still have family there?" Charley tried to picture his parents and guess at their concern for their footloose son.

Shad paused for the briefest of seconds then shook his head. "No." His glance lifted from his plate to her, a frown of curious interest in his expression. "How long have you and your brother been running this place alone?"

"Since we lost dad two years ago to a massive heart attack." The passing of time had allowed her to speak of her father's death with only a minor twinge of grief. "Our mother died five years before that, from pneumonia. Dad was never quite the same after she was gone."

"So now it's just you and Gary."

"Yes." She snapped a strip of crisp bacon in two and began munching on the smaller half.

"And neither of you have plans to enlarge the family circle." His chiseled mouth crooked in a doubting line. "I still find it difficult to believe you don't have a boyfriend somewhere in the fringes of your life. It doesn't seem natural."

Charley shrugged, aware of the flurry of her pulse as the conversation began to focus on her love life. "I'm sorry, but I'm not seriously interested in anyone."

"Ah." It was a smooth, knowing sound and his eyes danced with it. "That's the key to the puzzle, isn't it? You may not be 'seriously interested' in any man, but there undoubtedly is someone who is interested in you."

She considered denying it, but to what purpose?

"All right, yes," she admitted with a vaguely challenging look. "So far I haven't been able to convince him that I only care about him as a good friend and neighbor.... He thinks I'm one of those silly females who doesn't know her own mind. As long as he's patient and persistent, he figures that sooner or later I'll come to my senses."

"He's your neighbor?" The rising inflection of his voice made it a question.

41

Her nod was affirmative. "Chuck Weatherby. He owns the adjoining ranch."

In her mind's eye she pictured her would-be suitor. Pushing forty, he was of average height, his stocky build developing a paunch. Unlike Shad, hours in the sun had not given Chuck Weatherby a dark tan; rather, the fair complexion that went with his auburn hair had given him a perpetual sunburn. He was a good, solid man with unwavering loyalty and unquestionable devotion. There were many qualities about the man that Charley could admire, but he didn't spark any romantic interest. His kiss didn't stir her senses the way Shad's had a little while ago.

"Chuck Weatherby," Shad repeated the name and followed it with a throaty chuckle. "Chuck and Charley?"

An amused smile broke across her expression, laughing, too, at the combination of their similar names. "It sounds ridiculous, doesn't it?"

"I think a person could safely say it's unusual," he agreed with a quirking smile. "What is your given name? Charlotte or Charlene?"

"Charlotte, but practically no one ever calls me that. It's always Charley." She gave a little shrug that showed she had no objections to it and took a sip of her coffee.

"That's because it suits you." His gaze traveled over her in a way that seemed to take some of her breath. "A masculine-sounding name always makes a woman seem more feminine. The reverse isn't true, however. It would never work if your brother, Gary, was called Mary."

"Not hardly," she agreed dryly.

"I'm surprised your brother isn't married by now. A young, good-looking rancher should be a likely candidate for the single girls in the area," Shad commented, eyeing her with silent question.

"I suppose he is," Charley conceded. "A year ago he was almost out of circulation but the engagement was broken. Since then he's sworn off women."

"That's a noble vow, but it won't last." He seemed to speak from experience as he pushed his empty plate back and set his coffee cup in front of him. "What went wrong? Do you know?"

She shook her head, the mass of caramel-colored hair brushing her shoulders. "Gary doesn't like to talk about it." She wasn't sure if she should have even told Shad about it. He was virtually a stranger and here she was spilling the family secrets. Of course, Gary's broken engagement wasn't exactly a secret. It was the discovery that she was talking more freely to Shad than she did with most people that she found disconcerting. "How about you?" Charley switched the subject. "Have you ever been close to the marriage altar?"

"No, I haven't even been close enough to catch the scent of orange blossoms." Shad smiled at the question and took a swig of his coffee.

Charley realized she had been subconsciously wondering if a woman had started him out on his wandering path. It had seemed logical to assume he was running from something, but apparently that wasn't the case.

Silence stretched for a span of several seconds, broken by the scrape of a chair leg on the tiled kitchen floor as Shad came to his feet with lithe ease. Her upraised glance encountered the smiling light in his blue eyes.

"It's time I started earning my keep."

"Thanks for fixing breakfast. It was good."

"So was the company. Food always tastes better when you don't have to eat alone. I know," he said with a wry twist of his mouth.

That last comment of personal knowledge caused Charley to fall silent. As he turned away from the table she studied his lean, muscular form, the width of his shoulders tapering to a slim waist and hips, moving with the loose-limbed ease of a horseman. He paused at the back door to take his brown Stetson from the brass hook and push it onto the midnight black of his hair.

As he walked out the door without looking back she tried to imagine what the life of a drifter was like—traveling down so many lonely roads and meeting a lot of people, but never staying long enough to call any of them "friend." To her it seemed depressing, yet Shad always had a trace of humor in his expression. He seemed to be a vital and vigorous man, embracing life and living it to the fullest.

Still Charley sensed he was searching for something. Perhaps it was a place to call home. The thought brought a vague stirring of hope, which she quickly squashed. It wasn't wise to dream of such things. That led to a fast road to heartbreak with the drifting kind like Shad Russell.

While she nibbled on the last slice of toast, she cleared the table and stacked the dishes in the sink. The uneven thump of a pair of crutches heralded her brother's approach to the kitchen. Charley glanced over her shoulder as he entered the room.

"You're up early this morning." Since he'd come home from the hospital, he'd been in the habit of sleeping until nearly eight.

"My leg was bothering me," he explained and she could see the whiteness of discomfort in his tanned face. He paused inside the room, leaning his weight on the crutches. "I thought I smelled bacon. What did you do—eat without me?" His gaze centered on the dirty dishes in the sink where Charley was standing.

"Yes. Shad fixed breakfast this morning. For a change I got to eat somebody else's cooking besides my own." She moved away from the sink as Gary hobbled toward the table.

"Shad fixed breakfast?" he repeated with questioning surprise. While Charley held the chair steady, Gary lowered himself into it.

"Yes. You should take a lesson from him," she chided and scooted a second chair closer so he could prop his broken leg on it.

"Maybe he has discovered that's the way to a woman's heart," Gary suggested, surveying her with an inspecting look that Charley couldn't quite meet.

"I doubt it."

She laughed aside the suggestion, but the idea nagged her that Shad might have been trying to work his way into her good graces after she had tried to make it clear she wanted no physical involvement with him. "He was fixing his own breakfast so he could get an early start. When I came down he just threw another egg in the skillet for me."

"Maybe it wasn't such a good idea to hire this drifter," Gary murmured thoughtfully.

"What makes you say that?" As she started for the refrigerator to get his bacon and eggs she sent her brother a curious look.

"He's a good-looking devil, and even though you know your way around, you haven't had what could be described as an overabundance of male company lately. The two of you are going to be working together and living in the same house. You are not an unattractive woman, Charley. Sooner or later he's going to make a pass at you. And I'll lay you odds that he's the kind that loves 'em and leaves 'em."

She didn't dismiss her brother's words of caution. All she had to do was remember the sensations that had flowed through her when Shad had kissed her early this morning. There was a volatile chemistry between them, something she had to be on guard against. She chose not to mention the incident to Gary. Nor did she question his assessment of Shad's character. It was too close to her own opinion.

"As you said, Gary—" she shrugged to fake a lack of concern "—I'm old enough to take care of myself."

BUT SHAD'S PRESENCE in the household and the experience of the first day did alter Charley's routine. In the mornings she splashed cold water onto her face until she was fully awake before she went downstairs dressed for the day. And she was the one who fixed breakfast.

They were subtle precautions. Yet circumstances necessitated that she spend time in his company, working, sharing a meal, or spending the evening hours with him. The impact of his male vigor and ready smile didn't lessen with repeated exposure to it. In fact there were times when Charley felt her resistance was gradually being worn away. When his gaze would light on her with a glimmer of appreciation in their depths, she would feel a surge of satisfaction. Any direct contact with him, however accidental, would start a curious curling sensation in her toes. Those were the times when she wondered if she was waging a losing battle.

LESS THAN A WEEK after Shad had come to work for them, Charley was in the barn giving the horses their evening portion of grain. Outside she heard the rattle and roar of the tractor and mower signaling Shad's return from the hay field. She glanced at her wristwatch since Shad had told her at noon that he wouldn't be coming in until all the hay was cut. She had planned supper for seven; an oven meal of baked ham, scalloped potatoes and baked beans since those dishes would be the easiest to keep warm if Shad had worked until dark. As it was, by the time she finished with the evening chores and put the food on the table, Shad would have time to shower and clean up before sitting down to supper.

When the horses were grained, Charley tossed some hay into the corral and checked the water in the stock tank. The bay gelding, Dollar, nuzzled her shoulder, trying to wheedle an extra portion of grain from her. Charley laughed and rubbed its velvet nose.

"Sorry, fellah. That's all for tonight."

Slipping between the corral rails, she crawled through the fence and started toward the house. The grinding noise of a dead engine trying to be cranked to life attracted her attention. The sound stopped as she turned to locate its source and heard the tinny slam of a truck door. She changed her course, angling toward the machine shed where Shad was lifting the hood of an old pickup that had given up the ghost more than a year ago. She watched as he bent to examine the innards of the truck.

"It won't run." She approached him from the left, drawing his sideways glance.

"I noticed," Shad replied on a dryly amused note and went back to his inspection of the motor and its related parts.

"Any objections if I tinker around with it in my spare time?"

"Gary said it would cost more than it was worth to fix it," she warned. "He's been going to junk it, but hasn't got around to it yet."

"I'll pay for whatever spare parts are needed." He straightened to close the hood. His face and clothes were dusted with hay chaff and dirt, perspiration caking his clothes to his skin. "I'm in need of transportation. If I manage to get it running again, you can sign the pickup over to me in lieu of a month's wages."

"But what will you do for money?" Charley frowned.

"I have enough cash to get by," he insisted and held out his hand to shake on the bargain. "Is it a deal?"

"Unless Gary has some objections, it's a deal as far as I'm concerned," Charley agreed and let her hand become lost in the firm grip of his.

He held it a little longer than was necessary, his gaze locking with hers for a breath-stopping second.

When he let go of her hand, she tried to defuse the suddenly charged atmosphere. "I'm afraid you've landed yourself with a white elephant." She softly laughed out the remark, conscious of the musky smell of him, intensified by the heat of the sun and his body.

"One man's junk is another man's treasure," he shrugged and smiled. "Were you headed for the house?"

"Yes," she nodded.

"I'll walk with you."

He fell into step beside her as she started for her original destination. Her heart began skipping beats in schoolgirl fashion. It didn't resume its normal pace until they separated company inside the house when Shad went upstairs to shower and change.

CHAPTER THREE

FARMERS AND RANCHERS are rarely able to celebrate holidays or observe the Sabbath if there is work to be done in the fields or on the range. For a change, this Sunday in June was a day of rest on the Collins's ranch, except for the daily chores. The mowed hay in the fields was still too damp to be baled; none of the animals were sick; and no fences were down.

Charley had gone to the little community church in the mountains where she and Gary were members. Gary had refused to go with her, insisting that he wasn't going to ruin his one good pair of suit pants by cutting off one of the legs in order to put them on over his bulky cast. Shad had declined to attend, as well, without giving a reason. So Charley had gone without them, leaving instructions to keep an eye on the roast in the oven.

When she returned a little after twelve noon, the food was done and the table was set. Gary freely admitted that the credit belonged to Shad. The three of them sat down to a leisurely Sunday dinner with all the trimmings.

Not surprisingly, Charley didn't have any volunteers to help with the washing up. Shad disappeared outside and Gary clumped to the living room couch to lie down and take an afternoon nap. Even after the dishes were washed, dried, and put away, Charley still had the feeling she was a stuffed sausage with all the food she'd consumed. She went outside to walk off some of the fullness.

The serrated outline of the Sawtooth Mountains was etched sharply against the backdrop of a summer blue sky as Charley stepped from the front porch. She lifted her gaze to the distant peaks, a parade of rocky spires on the horizon. Their craggy tops were crowned with snow while thick pine forests blackened their slopes. At their feet, the lush rolling meadows of the high country valley sprawled, crisscrossed with mountain-fed streams and dressed in the green of early summer. The boundaries of the Collins's ranch lay within the valley floor in the shadow of the Sawtooth Mountains.

A breeze, fresh with the scent of pines, swept across the ranch yard and playfully tugged at the fold of her wraparound skirt, like a child eager to have her follow it. Charley smiled and let herself be urged along its path. It carried her first to the corrals where the horses trotted to the fence to see if she'd brought them any treats and stayed, crowding together and jealously vying for her attention.

After a little while she strolled away keeping to the relatively smooth ground of the ranch yard to make the walking easier in the spiky heels of her dress sandals. Shad was working on the old pickup truck, parked in the shade of the machine shed. Charley wandered over to see what progress he was making, if any. He was lying half under the front of the truck, limiting her view of him to the denim-clad, lower half of his body.

"Have you found out what's wrong with it yet?" Charley sidestepped the assortment of tools on the ground and stopped by the front fender.

"Yeah." Shad's voice was slightly muffled. "It won't run."

Charley laughed and countered with a

response as facetious as his own. "How clever of you to notice!"

Lying on his back, he scooted out from under the truck except for one shoulder. Her pulse was stimulated by the sight of his shirtless torso. His flatly muscled chest was all hard sinew and bone with a sprinkling of tightly curling black hair in a vee-shaped patch. The smearing stain of grease coated his large work-roughened hands. When she met his blue glance, there was a vibrancy to his look that tugged at her breath.

"I thought it was a rather brilliant deduction myself."

The lazy smile matched the mood of his drawling voice, while the shimmer of male interest was evident in his sweeping inspection of her. "Are you just going to stand there and be ornamental or will you pass me that wrench?"

Bending her knees, Charley stooped beside the assortment of tools and picked up a wrench. "This one?"

At his affirmative nod, she handed it to him and remained in her crouched position, half-sitting on her heels to peer under the truck to watch him as he worked. She was entranced by the rippling play of straining muscles as he labored to loosen an unseen bolt. She folded her hands across her knees, letting the hem of her skirt drag the ground.

Without pausing in his efforts, he let his glance run back to her for a brief instant. "Has anyone ever told you that you have a beautiful pair of legs?"

Since her skirt was hiding them now, Charley guessed that he must have noticed them before, when she was standing. Her legs tingled in delayed reaction, as if only now becoming aware of the stroking of his admiring gaze.

"Not lately." But she wasn't sure that anyone had ever mentioned they thought she had attractive legs.

"It's a shame they spend so much time covered by a pair of jeans." Shad remarked. With the bolt loosened by the wrench, he spun it free with his fingers. "That part's done." The ring of accomplishment was in his voice as he wormed his way out from under the truck and passed Charley the wrench.

In reaching for it, she misjudged the distance and slid her hand over his dirt-and-grease-coated fingers. The contact left a smear of grime on the side of her hand. Charley didn't notice it until she had replaced the wrench. As she was straightening to an erect position, Shad was rolling to his feet in a move of superb coordination.

"Do you have a rag?" she asked when she saw the black smear. "I got grease on myself."

"There's one on the left fender." He indicated its location with a wave of his hand.

As she walked over and picked it up, a vagrant breeze whipped a thick length of sandy hair across her face and into her eyes. Half-blinded, she unconsciously used her dirty hand to push it out of her eyes and unknowingly left a dark streak of grease across her cheekbone. When she could see clearly again, she began scrubbing her hand with the rag.

"You've smeared it on your cheek," Shad pointed out, a smile edging the corners of his mouth as he studied her.

"I have?" She lifted clean fingers to her cheek and brushed them over the prominent bone. They came away with traces of the dirty grease. When she tried to wipe her cheek clean with the cloth rag, she only succeeded in spreading the grease.

"You'd better let me do it," he stated and took the rag from her hand, encountering only hesitant resistance.

His male lips lay flat against each other, held straight, but slashing smile lines were in his lean cheeks and slanting from his eyes. He folded the cloth until he had exposed a clean square patch.

The task demanded that he stand very close to her. Charley felt the acceleration of her heartbeat as she lifted her face to his ministrations.

He wiped at the smear with firm, even strokes, taking his time to erase the smallest particle. She could see the pores of his skin and the black centers of his vibrantly blue eyes, half-closed as they looked down at her face. Her breathing was shallow, affected by his nearness and the raw, male vitality that flowed from him. Charley lowered her gaze, fighting the powerful attraction he exerted on her. The sight of the sun-bronzed wall of his bare chest was equally undermining in its influence on her senses. When she looked up again, his gaze was centered on her lips with disturbing intensity. It produced an aching tightness in her throat.

Regardless of the way her body was reacting, she wasn't a giddy teenager anymore. Although she didn't claim to be worldly-wise, she knew the score. It didn't matter how it was added up, she would wind up being the loser in a romantic encounter with this man.

"Stop it, Shad." Her voice was low and husky with control.

"Stop what?" His look was alive with male interest, boldly sensual and disarming.

"Stop looking at me like that." She kept her reply steady and faked a calmness.

"Like what?" He pretended an interest in her smeared cheek, but Charley was certain it had been wiped away long ago. "Like I wanted to make love to you?" He rephrased the question to be more specific.

Charley tried to ignore the tumbling rush of her heart. "Yes," she said evenly.

"Does it bother you?" His mouth quirked, mocking her with the devilry of his smile.

"I'm as human as you are, Shad, but I'm not a fool," she replied and moved out of his reach, trying to conceal the tremors that rocked her.

But he made no attempt to lessen the distance as he began wiping his greasy hands on the cloth. "Because I'm only passing through." He guessed her reason for backing off from the possibility of an embrace.

"Aren't you?" She challenged him to deny it.

A hint of a frown flickered across his expression as he half turned away to throw the rag onto the truck hood. His split-second hesitation before answering caused Charley to hold her breath. But he gave her the reply she had initially expected.

"I'll be moving on sooner or later," Shad admitted without apology or any show of regret.

The ranch was nothing more than a stopgap in his travels. She meant nothing special to him. He was only attracted to her because she was on the scene and available. Charley had guessed all this but there was no satisfaction in having her suspicions confirmed. One foolish segment of her heart was wishing he had lied.

Her gaze lingered on his averted face and watched the breeze rumple his heavy black hair. When he turned his head to meet her look, she felt the throb of tension in the air. It was broken by the powerful drone of an approaching car. They both glanced at the intruder on the scene as the car entered the ranch yard.

"It looks like you have a visitor," Shad remarked with cool indifference.

Charley had recognized the late-model Buick slowing to a stop near the house and would have passed the information along to him if he had shown the least amount of interest. But he had turned his back to her, his attention reverting to the partially dismantled truck motor.

There was taut pressure in the line of her mouth as she started forward to greet the stocky man climbing out of the cream-colored Buick. She forced it into a curving smile of welcome when she came closer to him.

"Hello, Chuck," she greeted the owner of the

neighboring ranch, her most patient and persistent admirer.

He took off his beige, felt Stetson in a gesture of old-fashioned deference to the presence of a woman. His white dress shirt emphasized the broadness of his thickening waist. A heavy silver buckle inlaid with turquoise protruded with his stomach. His face was ruddy from constant exposure to the sun except for a white streak across the top of his forehead where his hat had protected it. By no stretch of the imagination did he cut a dashing figure, yet he was innately good and kind—and devoted to Charley. His deep affection for her glowed with a gentle light from his brown eyes.

"Hello, Charley," he returned the greeting and added, "You look lovely today."

"Thank you." It was strange how a compliment from Chuck Weatherby meant nothing to her. Yet if Shad had told her that, she would have beamed inwardly with pleasure.

"Am I interrupting anything?" he asked, then explained, "I was out for a drive and took the chance that you weren't busy to stop by to find out how you are."

"You aren't interrupting anything," Charley assured him. In fact she secretly felt he couldn't have come at a better time. She had been strongly tempted by Shad's company. "I was just walking off my Sunday dinner."

"Who is the man you were talking to when I drove in? I don't think I recognize him." He frowned as he glanced in Shad's direction.

She followed his gaze and felt a surge of reluctant admiration at the sight of Shad's muscled physique. A sheen of perspiration made his hard flesh glisten like polished bronze in the encroaching sunlight.

Charley attempted a casual reply to the inquiry. "That's our new hired hand."

"He isn't local," Chuck stated and sent her a questioning look.

"No, he isn't. His name is Shad Russell—from Colorado, originally." She realized what scant information they possessed about him, little beyond his name and previous employers. All a rancher needed to know about a man was whether or not he could do the job. She was curious about his past only because she was beginning to develop a personal interest in him.

"A drifter." The disapproval of the breed was obvious in the tone of Chuck's voice. "I thought you and your brother were going to hire someone local to help out."

"There wasn't anyone available," Charley explained with an unconcerned shrug.

"You should have got hold of me." He gave her a reproving glance. "I could have spared one of my men to help you this summer."

"Then you would have been shorthanded, Chuck. No, this way is better." She turned down his belated suggestion, because she didn't want to be under any obligation to their neighbor no matter how well intentioned it was. She would have felt she owed him something even if Chuck wouldn't.

He didn't try to argue with her but his look narrowed with displeasure on Shad. "Your brother needs to have a talk with that man. A man shouldn't be taking his shirt off to work when there is a woman present. It isn't proper."

"I imagine he didn't want to ruin his shirt with grease and oil from that old truck. Besides, it doesn't offend me." Charley was careful not to smile at Chuck's criticism and silently wondered if he wasn't perhaps a little envious of Shad's virile form. There wasn't an ounce of fat on Chuck's frame. It was simply that his muscles had settled around his middle! She doubted that Chuck had ever been built like Shad, even when he was younger.

"I still say it shows a lack of respect," he insisted stubbornly.

"It's getting warm out here in the sun." With

a change of subject, she directed his attention away from Shad. "Let's go in the house and have a cold drink." As she started to move toward the house Chuck was quick to follow.

"I know you want to chat with Gary while you're here."

"Yes, of course, I do." His quick reply told her what she already knew. He hadn't stopped to see her brother. It was her company he wanted. "How is he?"

"Much better."

Gary was sound asleep on the couch, snoring his way through a rick of logs when they entered the house. Charley ignored Chuck's protests not to disturb him and shook her brother's shoulder to waken him. He stirred groggily, then spied their guest and pushed himself into a sitting position. Charley plumped some pillows and positioned them against the armrest to support his back so Gary could keep his broken leg stretched on the couch.

Gary stifled a yawn with his hand and smiled sleepily at his neighbor. "What brings you over here, Chuck?"

"I just wanted to see how you were getting along." Chuck Weatherby lowered his stocky frame into the armchair that matched the blue-flowered sofa.

"Oh?" Gary slid a knowing glance at Charley. "I thought it might have been my sister that you came to see."

She buried her brother with a killing smile. "I'm going to fix a cold drink. What would you like? Lemonade or iced tea?" Both men chose lemonade and she excused herself to go to the kitchen. "It will only take me a few minutes."

As always happened whenever the two ranchers were left alone together, they became embroiled in a discussion of ranching, the livestock market, the effects of the weather, and this year versus previous years. It was something Charley had counted on and she wasn't disappointed when she returned to the living room to serve them their glasses of iced lemonade.

While they talked around her, she strategically placed coasters on the coffee table in front of the sofa so the walnut finish wouldn't be marred by water rings. Then she relaxed in the gold recliner with her glass of lemonade and raised the footrest. Chuck didn't expect a woman to be knowledgeable about the subjects they were discussing, so she wasn't obliged to take part in the conversation. Charley was content to sit in the chair and let the talk flow around her.

After about an hour the conversation digressed to the topic of politics. Charley day-dreamed through most of it until she heard someone come in the back door of the kitchen. Aware that it had to be Shad, she stirred from the reclining lounge chair. Her movement attracted Chuck's attention and she received a questioning look.

"With all this dry talk, I thought you might like some more lemonade," she said.

He glanced at his empty glass and nodded. "Yes, I would."

"I'll bring in the pitcher." She quietly exited the room.

Shad was standing at the sink when she entered the kitchen. He turned sideways to glance at her as she approached. He had put his shirt on but hadn't bothered to button it or tuck it inside his Levi's. It hung loose, giving her a glimpse of his bare chest. Swinging back to the sink, he turned on the cold-water faucet and let it run while he took a glass from the cupboard.

"I fixed a pitcher of lemonade," Charley said as she walked to the refrigerator.

"No, thanks. I prefer water." Shad filled a glass and drank it down, then turned to lean a hip against the sink counter and watch her. "Did your boyfriend come acourting this afternoon?" He nodded in the direction of the living room.

"He isn't my boyfriend, but, yes, it is Chuck Weatherby from the next ranch," Charley admitted.

"If he isn't your boyfriend, it isn't from lack of trying," he observed dryly and ran more water into his glass.

She didn't see any reason to argue the point. "You're welcome to join us."

"It's only a guess, but I'd say your friend wouldn't like it." His mouth slanted in a wry line. "So thanks for the invitation, but I think I'll pass."

Charley didn't try to change his mind because she knew he was right. His presence would irritate Chuck. With the pitcher of lemonade in hand, she returned to the living room. Stopping first near Chuck's chair, she picked up his glass to fill it with the lemonade. He tipped his head in her direction.

"Did I hear you talking to someone in the kitchen?" he asked.

"Yes. Shad came in for a drink of water," she admitted offhandedly to downplay any significance. Replacing Chuck's glass on its coaster, she glanced at her brother. "More lemonade?"

"No, thanks," he refused.

Charley refilled her glass then carried the

pitcher back to the kitchen. While she had been out of the room, Shad had slipped quietly out of the back door. She glanced out the window and saw him crossing the yard to the machine shed. Fighting the twinge of disappointment, she returned the pitcher to the refrigerator shelf and rejoined Chuck and her brother in the living room. She quietly resumed her listening post in the recliner chair.

When the Black Forest cuckoo clock on the wall sang out half-past four, it roused Charley from her chair. "I didn't realize it was so late. It's time I started supper." She politely hinted that it was time Chuck left, but her brother thwarted it.

"Why don't you stay and eat with us, Chuck?" he invited.

Charley could have screamed. She tried to catch her brother's eye but he wouldn't look at her. Meanwhile Chuck was silently debating whether or not to accept.

"No. I'd better be getting home," he said finally, and Charley nearly sighed aloud with relief. When he turned to look at her, she fixed a bright expression on her face. "I did want to invite you to have dinner with me Friday night."

"I don't know," she stalled, seeking an adequate excuse to refuse. "We'll be baling hay all this week. I'll probably be too tired. Besides, I wouldn't like to leave Gary alone."

"Nonsense!" her brother scoffed at that reason. "I'm not an invalid. All I have is a broken leg, for heaven's sake. You've been under a lot of pressure lately. You need to go out for an evening and enjoy yourself."

"But who would feed you?" she argued, wishing he would keep his mouth shut.

"Fix a casserole. Something Shad and I could warm up," Gary reasoned with a twinkle in his eyes.

"It seems Gary has found a solution to your problems, Charley," Chuck inserted. "Will you come out to dinner with me on Friday?"

It appeared that she had little choice. "Yes." It was a clipped acceptance as she gave in to the pressure with ill grace.

A few minutes later, after Chuck had made arrangements to pick her up at six on Friday, he rose to leave. Charley walked him as far as the front door and watched him climb into his car and drive away. She was fuming when she turned to confront her brother.

"You really were a lot of help, Gary. With a brother like you, I don't need enemies," she snapped. "I've done everything but beat Chuck over the head trying to make him understand that I'm not interested in him. Then you go and force me into accepting a date with him."

"Be practical, Charley." He tried to calm her. "He wants to take you out and you need the outing, so what's wrong with taking advantage of the opportunity? It isn't committing you to anything."

"I happen to like Chuck as a person," she retorted. "And I don't think it's right to use him simply because he happens to be a convenient escort. It isn't fair to him." She turned on her heel and stalked into the kitchen, sorry that there wasn't a door to slam to vent some of her anger.

Charley was still seething when they all sat down to supper that night. The tension at the table was unmistakable. Sparks flew every time she looked at her brother. Shad eyed them both with a trace of humor.

"Is something wrong?" he asked finally.

Gary shrugged. "Charley's sulking because I forced her into accepting a date with Chuck this Friday. She hasn't been out of this house in weeks. I thought she needed to get away from here and let her hair down."

"I can't imagine letting my hair down with someone as conservative as Chuck," she retorted.

"Maybe not," her brother conceded. "But

you haven't exactly had a flood of invitations for dates lately. And beggars can't be choosers."

Fire burned in the look she gave Gary. "You're lucky I'm not sitting on the other side of the table, because I just might be tempted to rebreak that leg of yours."

"There's nothing quite like sisterly love." Her brother grinned at Shad.

An angry sound of exasperated disgust came from her throat as she rose from the table to fetch the dessert. There were times when her brother was absolutely impossible. Tonight was one of them.

THE WEEK THAT FOLLOWED WAS HECTIC, every minute filled from sunup to sundown. Charley fell into bed each night, totally exhausted, and dragged herself out of bed each morning. By Friday there didn't seem to be enough cold water to chase the sleep out of her eyes. Finally she gave up trying. She opened the bathroom door and walked straight into Shad.

"Oh." It was a soft sound of delayed shock as she found her arms resting against the solid wall of his chest. She swayed backward unsteadily, trembling from the unexpected contact with his warm flesh.

"Steady, girl." His hands closed on her

shoulders to give her balance. There was a smiling light in his blue eyes as they ran over her upturned face. His look disturbed her with its caressing quality. "We've got to stop meeting like this." His drawling voice lowered its pitch to an intimate level. "Good ole Chuck might get the wrong idea if he found out about it."

Stung by his mockery, Charley broke out of his light hold and quickly sidestepped him. "Don't be ridiculous," she declared in a voice low with anger. But he only chuckled. "I don't think it's funny," she said as she started toward her bedroom door.

His voice trailed after her. "Tonight's the big night, isn't it?"

She didn't think that remark was worthy of a response so she closed the door on him. Yet, in the quiet of her bedroom, the encounter outside the bathroom door started her thinking about how many things they shared besides a common bathroom. They ate at the same table, slept under the same roof, drank from the same water jug out in the hay fields. She had spent more time with Shad under a variety of circumstances than she had with any other man in her life except for her brother. It was an unsettling discovery to realize how much he'd become a part of her life in two short weeks.

CHAPTER FOUR

CHARLEY WAS READY promptly at six o'clock that evening when Chuck came to pick her up. She had left a casserole in the oven and salads in the refrigerator for Shad and her brother to have as their evening meal.

As they walked to his car she was conscious of Chuck's approving glance sweeping over her. The long-sleeved shirtlike dress was made out of a silky material, navy blue in color with white polka dots. It had a wide matching belt at the waistline and a flared skirt. It was one of the most flattering dresses she owned, its dark color a complement to her honey-colored hair. She wasn't sure but she thought she might have chosen it out of spite, dressing with care simply because she had been maneuvered into accepting a date she didn't want.

The evening spent with Chuck Weatherby wasn't the ordeal that Charley pretended it was going to be. He was an undemanding companion and it was easy to relax with him. She would have enjoyed it more if she hadn't been aware that he wanted their relationship to become something permanent and binding. If her conscience hadn't bothered her, it would have been a perfect evening.

After a long and leisurely meal at a restaurant in Ketchum, Charley wasn't surprised when Chuck suggested that he take her home. He wasn't the kind of person to stay out until all hours of the night, and with the exhausting week she'd had, she willingly agreed to his suggestion.

As they started out on the long drive back to the ranch Charley gazed out the window at the shimmer of stars in the night sky. They made the perfect backdrop for the magnificence of the moonlight-bathed mountain range. The combination of natural tiredness and the contentment of a good meal and pleasant company soon had Charley nodding off.

When she caught herself almost falling sound asleep, she sat up straighter in the car seat and glanced self-consciously at Chuck. There was a faint smile curving his mouth that indicated he had noticed her lapse.

"I'm sorry," she apologized. "I didn't realize I was so tired." Her eyelids felt as if there were lead weights attached to them.

"Use my shoulder for a pillow," Chuck offered. "Otherwise you'll end up with a crick in your neck."

"But, I—" She'd started to protest that she wouldn't fall asleep again when she was interrupted by a big yawn that refused to be postponed. She realized she was only kidding herself. She wouldn't stay awake for the entire ride. "Okay," she accepted his offer and shifted closer to lay her cheek on his shoulder. Almost immediately her eyes closed.

"You realize that we should be driving back to our own home." It was the first remark he'd made in a long while that intimated his desire for their future. Charley stiffened and would have spoken, but he went on. "No, don't say anything," he said. "I've heard it all before, but it doesn't change the way I feel about you, Charley. And I can't explain what it is that makes me be so certain that someday you will wear my ring. It's just a feeling I have. I guess that's why I won't give up even though you've made it clear that I'm wasting my time.'' Charley didn't know how to fill the silence that followed his statement. After a few minutes he said gently, "Go to sleep."

When she finally closed her eyes, she didn't open them again until the car slowed to a stop in the ranch yard. She sat up slowly, stretching her shoulders and blinking away the sleep in her eyes.

"Your brother left a light on in the house for you," Chuck observed as he turned off the motor.

Charley noticed it, too. "Why don't you come in for a little while and I'll fix some coffee?" she suggested.

He hesitated a split second, then accepted. "All right."

Before Chuck had a chance to climb out of the car and walk around to her side, she had the door open and was stepping out. He waited for her by the hood of the car and walked her to the house. The coolness of the mountain air was fresh and invigorating, chasing away the last remnants of sleepiness.

As she entered the house her gaze was automatically drawn to the lamp left burning. Shad was sitting in a chair beside it, illuminated by its pool of light. Although he was fully dressed, his large hands were busy with a shirt in his lap. He looked up when she entered, but Charley didn't notice. She was too busy staring at the glint of silver flashing in and out of the shirt material, certain her mind was playing tricks on her.

"I didn't expect you home so early," he said. "Gary went to bed about twenty minutes ago."

His voice broke the spell and she met his gaze, partially aware that Chuck was standing beside her. "What are you doing?"

"A button came off this shirt. I'm sewing it on," Shad replied in a tone that indicated it was the logical thing to do. "There's plenty of coffee still hot in the kitchen."

"Thank you." She glanced at Chuck and saw him eyeing Shad with a measuring look. She realized the two men hadn't formally met. "Chuck, this is Shad Russell, our new hired man. This is Chuck Weatherby, a fellow rancher and neighbor."

"No, don't get up." Chuck waved him back into the chair when Shad started to gather his sewing together to stand.

"You two probably want the living room to yourselves," Shad said. "I'll finish this in my room."

"Don't bother," Charley inserted quickly. "Chuck and I will have our coffee in the kitchen.'' When she glanced at Chuck to obtain his consent, she noticed his expression appeared oddly tight-lipped. He was usually good-natured and easygoing.

"That will be fine," he agreed with her suggestion.

She started to suggest that Shad have coffee with them, then bit her tongue just in time. After another glance at Chuck, she moved toward the kitchen while he trailed in her wake. The coffee smelled hot and fresh as she took two cups from the cupboard and filled them with coffee from the pot. She carried them to the kitchen table where Chuck was sitting.

"Do you take cream or sugar?" She didn't remember.

"Neither." His expression appeared grim. "Does that man sleep here in the house?" His voice was pitched low so it wouldn't carry into the living room.

She was startled by the question and a little bit angry at the implication that Shad wasn't fit to live under the same roof. "Where do you think he sleeps? In the barn with the animals? He sleeps in the spare bedroom upstairs."

"I don't like it." He picked up the cup and stared into the black liquid.

"You don't have to like it as long as Gary and

I are satisfied with the arrangements," she retorted.

"It's you I'm worried about, Charley," he explained. "It isn't proper for a strange man to be staying here with you."

"Perhaps it wouldn't be if I lived here alone, but my brother lives here, too, in case you've forgotten," she reminded him somewhat acidly. "My reputation is hardly in jeopardy."

"I don't think you understand my concern." There was a wealth of patience in his voice. "You are a very attractive woman. The proximity of living under the same roof with you is liable to give the man ideas."

Living in the same house with Shad was giving *her* ideas, but she couldn't very well tell Chuck that. "Please," she said wearily. "It was such a lovely evening. Let's don't end it by arguing."

Pausing, he appeared to consider her request before he responded. "You're right," he agreed and pushed his cup aside without having drunk any coffee. "Thanks for the coffee, but it's time I was getting home." As he stood up Charley started to do the same, but he forestalled her. "I'll show myself out."

Stopping at her chair, he crooked a finger under her chin and leaned down to kiss her good-night. He was not inexperienced. The pressure of his mouth was warm and ardent, but it left her unmoved. Charley saw the vague disappointment in his expression when he lifted his head and knew her response had been inadequate but she refused to fake what she didn't feel.

"Good night, Chuck," she murmured.

His smile was faintly sad as he left the kitchen. She remained at the table until she heard the front door close and his footsteps on the porch. She rose, leaving her coffee untouched, and slipped her hand into the silken pockets of her skirt to wander into the living room.

In the shadows near the front door she paused and listened to the car start and drive away. Her gaze was drawn to Shad, seated in the overstuffed chair. She watched his large hand using the slim needle with such deftness as it made the last few passes to secure the button to the shirt material. Tying a knot, he lifted the thread to his mouth and bit it in two.

"I would have sewed that button on for you," Charley drifted out of the shadows. "You didn't have to do it."

"You've spoiled me enough already." He pushed the silver needle into the strawberry pincushion and returned it to her sewing basket by the chair.

"How?" She tipped her head to one side, a heavy mass of tawny hair spilling over one shoulder. She didn't recall going out of her way to do anything special for him.

"Doing my laundry, fixing all those delicious home-cooked meals, and keeping my room clean," Shad replied, gliding to his feet in one motion.

She laughed softly and came closer. "That hardly constitutes being spoiled."

"Maybe not to some," he agreed with a slow smile. "How was your evening?"

"Fine." Charley gave a noncommittal answer because she didn't feel like talking about it. Aware of the penetrating study of his gaze, she avoided it.

"Didn't he kiss you good-night?" He sounded both curious and vaguely surprised.

She lifted her head, a little defiant. "Yes, he did."

Reaching out, he held her waist in his hands and maneuvered her into the lamplight so he could see her face clearly. The weight of his hands was heavy, holding her in place while his gaze wandered over her features.

"Funny. You don't look kissed," he said at

last. The pressure of his grip increased, pulling her slowly closer to him. His eyes seemed to change color, growing darker and becoming sober. His mouth began a slow descent, stopping before it reached her lips. While the warmth of his breath caressed her skin, she drank in the intoxicating smell of him, a combination of after-shave, soap, and that individual scent that was his alone. "Chuck is a good man. He'd make a wonderful husband and a loving father for your children. He would be good for you, Charley. You really should marry him."

It wasn't at all what she had expected him to say. She flashed him a surprised and irritated look. "Everyone keeps trying to throw me at Chuck. First Gary and now you. What is this—a conspiracy?" she protested, pulling an inch or so back from his face to glare at him. "Everyone wants me to marry him, but no one bothers to ask me what I want."

"I think I know what you want." His gaze centered on her lips. The desire that burned in his eyes stole her anger. "I'm no good for you, Charley. We both know it. But it doesn't seem to matter, does it? It doesn't change anything."

"No," she whispered and stopped listening to her common sense.

His mouth came down those last few inches to settle onto her lips with tantalizing ease. A sweet rush of forbidden joy ran through her veins as her hands slid around his neck and she melted into his arms. A steel band circled her waist to press her tighter to his length while his other hand tunneled under the thickness of her hair to cup the back of her head.

The driving hunger of his kiss parted her lips, giving him access to the most intimate recesses of her mouth. She was caught in a whirl of sensation, all golden and consuming. Her sensitive fingers were alive to the blunt texture of his hair. She was crushed against the hard contours of his lean body, her flesh throbbing at the muscled tautness of his.

A tiny cry of intense longing broke from her when the hotness of his mouth moved to her throat and burned a nuzzling path to her ear. He tugged at an earlobe with his teeth and teased a hollow with the tip of his tongue. The roughness of his breathing was no better controlled than her own. He lifted his head, pulling away to create a small space between them while his hand absently rubbed the small of her back.

"Where do we go from here, Charley?" It was a low, husky query. "You tell me."

Unwillingly she opened her eyes and looked

down the road. Eventually he would leave her. She knew it as certainly as she knew her own name. She pulled her hands from around his neck and pushed at his forearms to end their encirclement of her. It cost her a lot to deny him.

"We don't go anywhere from here," she said, "not together."

Shad accepted her answer with a trace of fatalism. Withdrawing his arms from around her, he raised a hand to cup the side of her face in his palm. A calloused thumb brushed her lips, tracing their moist and swollen outline.

"At least now you look like you've been kissed." His mouth quirked in a mocking line.

His hand fell away as he stepped back, setting her free. Charley hesitated uncertainly, then walked to the staircase. She paused at the opening to look back, but Shad was already disappearing into the kitchen. She slowly climbed the stairs to her bedroom.

THE WEEKEND CAME AND WENT with Charley trying to pretend that nothing earth-shattering had happened and attempting to pickup the threads of her previously friendly relationship with Shad. He appeared to accept her Friday night answer as final but there continued to be an awareness of her in his eyes although he didn't make any overt moves. But Charley was discovering that the daily exposure to him was only increasing the attraction.

Gary had mastered the use of his crutches. He could do anything and go anywhere on them. No longer housebound, he began doing some of the light chores such as feeding the horses, thus freeing Charley and Shad of that responsibility.

With the dawn of Thursday morning, Charley wakened to discover a steady rain was falling. There would be no ranch work done except the daily chores that Shad took care of. Charley used most of the morning cleaning the house. The kitchen was the last room on her list. Gary was sitting at the table with his leg propped on a chair when she entered.

"Did you hear that?" he asked.

"Hear what?" She half frowned as she glanced at him, her mind busy trying to decide what to fix for lunch. Then, above the steady rainfall, she heard the sputtering cough of an engine before it caught and roared to life. Charley didn't understand the significance of that sound until Gary explained.

"Shad has been working on that old truck this morning. It sounds as if he's got it running." He shook his head in wry amazement. "I didn't think he could do it. He's really something, isn't he?"

"Yes." It wasn't a subject she could comfortably discuss. He was becoming much too special in her life. She walked to the refrigerator. "How about cold roast beef sandwiches for lunch?"

"What you're trying to tell me is that we're going to have leftovers for lunch," Gary said dryly.

"I want to clean the refrigerator this afternoon," she defended her position.

"Bring on the leftovers," he declared with a motioning wave of his hand.

Charley began carrying the plastic food containers from the refrigerator to the table, an assortment of condiments and dressings, and a loaf of bread from the bread drawer. As she got out the plates and silverware the hum of the truck engine seemed nearer. She even thought she heard the tires splashing in the puddles of water. A horn blared right outside the kitchen door, causing her to jump. It sent out its summons a second time and Charley set the plates and silverware on the table and hurried to the back door.

Gary was a fraction slower, reaching the door after she had opened it. The truck was stopped just outside, the motor idling as steadily as a purring cat. Shad had rolled the window down on the driver's side and had an arm hooked over the frame. A hand was resting on the steering wheel. His lean, rugged features were broken with a wide smile, his blue eyes dancing with a thousand lights.

"It sounds great!" Gary told him.

"Thanks!" But his attention was focused on Charley, disarming with its slightly laughing persuasion. "Let's go for a ride, Charley!"

"I just put lunch on the table." She lifted her shoulders in an expression of genuine regret, ensnared by his celebrative mood.

"So?" he grinned. "Let Gary eat it." His gaze sliced to her brother. "Promise you won't break your neck if we leave you alone for a couple hours."

"I promise." Gary mockingly crossed his heart in a childhood vow.

"Come on, Charley," Shad coaxed.

She glanced sideways at her brother, who smiled and gave an approving nod. "Go on."

She needed no second urging as she dashed out from beneath the shelter of the overhang and into the raindrops. Shad had leaned across the seat and opened the passenger door for her so she could climb right in.

"Are you sure this thing doesn't leak?" She was slightly out of breath as she slid onto the seat and closed the door.

"Does a Rolls-Royce leak?" He gave her a look of mock reproval that she should have so little faith in the old truck. "Of course not."

As he shifted the truck into forward gear a huge drop of water plopped onto the dashboard and they broke into laughter simultaneously. Charley reached out to wipe it away with the sleeve of her plaid blouse.

"A little water never hurt anyone," Charley assured him.

"That's what I thought." He sent a saluting wave to Gary standing in the back doorway and started the truck rolling forward. The windshield wipers swished back and forth, leaving spotty patches of water where the blades failed to touch the glass.

"You need new windshield wipers," she pointed out.

"But only when it rains," he countered with a wickedly teasing look.

"What do you think it's doing now?" she laughed.

"That's only liquid sunshine," he insisted.

As he turned the truck around in the yard and headed it down the lane, she felt the smooth acceleration of power. "It really runs well, better than before it quit working."

"All it needed was some loving attention and a few well-chosen words." A dark eyebrow arched with speaking amusement and Charley recalled a few times when she'd heard him cussing out a resisting engine part.

She laughed and lifted a hand to fluff the rain-dampened hair around her face. The quick dash from the house to the truck had left her only slightly wet. She would dry quickly.

"Now you have your own transportation," she declared. "When you finally leave, you won't have to hitchhike. You can drive away in your own truck." Almost as soon as the words were out, she regretted them. Just knowing the day would come brought a twinge of pain in her midsection. She wished she hadn't referred to it.

"That's right." Even the lightness of his voice sounded forced.

Leaning back in the seat, she let her head rest on the curved top and turned her gaze out the window. The mountains were shrouded in dark clouds, a gray mist hanging over the valley floor. The tap-tapping of the rain on the metal roof of the truck was a soothing sound.

"I love to ride in the rain," Charley said.

"So do I," Shad agreed and slowed the truck

as they reached the intersection with the highway. There was no traffic in sight and he pulled onto the road.

"Where did you learn so much about fixing engines?" She was curious about how he had become so knowledgeable about so many things.

"I picked it up here and there, just like everything else. An old Mexican showed me how to braid and make cinch straps as soft as velvet when I worked on a ranch in Arizona. And an old-timer in Wyoming showed me a few tricks with a rope. You can learn a lot of things if you keep your eyes and ears open." His sideways glance held humor "*And*—as long as you're not ashamed to admit that you're ignorant about something."

Yet it seemed to her that he was letting all his knowledge and abilities go to waste. She didn't understand why he had remained a drifter, never using his intelligence to make something better out of his life.

"Haven't you ever wanted to be something else than what you are?" she frowned. She face his profile, her cheek resting on the back of the seat.

"Something other than a cowboy?" He named his profession, then silently shook his head. "Granted the hours are long. Sometimes it seems that you get up so early in the morning that you're eating breakfast in the middle of the night. And the work is hard, sometimes dirty and smelly. The pay is cheap. A guy could earn a lot more working in a factory in the city. But it's a proud way to live."

There was an underlying emphasis on the last sentence, a sense of deep satisfaction and— pride. Charley was moved by the force of his abiding love for his profession and was sorry she had implied it wasn't a worthy one.

"Was you father a cowboy, too?" Giving way to her curiosity, she unconsciously began to delve into his background.

"I really don't know." He spared her a glance, his expression vaguely thoughtful as he met her confused and questioning look after such a strange answer. He smiled absently and let his attention return to the highway. "I was abandoned as a child when I was some- where around two years old. I don't remember anything about my natural parents. There weren't any papers left with me. I have no idea when or where I was born or what my real name is."

"I see," Charley murmured as a picture began to form in her mind. "This was in Colorado?'' She remembered he had told her that was where he had been raised.

''Yes.'' The rain had become spotty and Shad switched off the windshield wipers.

''Didn't they try to find your parents?'' It seemed incomprehensible to her that someone could abandon their child. She wondered what kind of people could do that, and guessed the same thought had probably occurred to Shad. Such an experience had to leave a scar.

''They tried,'' he said with an expressive shrug, a certain impassivity about his features. ''A service-station owner found me sleeping in one of the rest rooms when he opened up for business one morning. There wasn't any clue to go on. The station had been closed so no one saw who left me. There was always the chance my parents would come back to claim me so I wasn't considered adoptable. I was shuffled from one foster home to another.''

''So you never really knew what it was like to have a family,'' Charley realized. Traveling, always moving on, had been a part of his lifestyle from a very early age. There hadn't been a stable home in his life.

''Not in the beginning,'' he admitted, and sent her a smiling look that held no self-pity. ''None of my foster parents ever mistreated me.

They were all good to me but I was still an outsider. It wasn't until I was older that I discovered most children had parents and a family. When I found out differently, I was realistic enough not to cry about something I couldn't change. In some ways I was lucky because I was exposed to a variety of environments and lifestyles, learned a lot about people, and life in general.''

''But it had to have an effect on you,'' Charley insisted.

''I learned to be self-reliant and independent. ''I struck out on my own when I was seventeen,'' he explained. ''I got a job herding sheep up in the high country of Colorado with a Basque shepherd as my partner. From there I went to work for a quarter-horse breeder, cleaning stables. Cattle were a sideline with him. That's where I started riding fence and working branding crews. I moved south after that— Arizona, New Mexico, Texas. I've seen a lot of country.'' His gaze made a sweep of the rugged land outside the truck windows. ''But I guess I was mountain-bred. Look at that.''

With absent obedience, she glanced out the window and felt the breath being drawn from her lungs. It had stopped raining, leaving behind a world that had been washed clean. The air was vibrantly clear and fresh, its clean scent rushing into the cab through the now opened windows. The leaves of the trees had seemed to turn emerald green, while the pines took on the darker shade of green. The sun had broken through the clouds, a patch of blue showing in the sky. Against the backdrop of the wild mountains, a rainbow arched its multicolored promise.

"Everything is always so beautiful after a rain," Charley murmured with a trace of awe.

"Yes." But he was looking straight at her when he said it. The disturbing darkness of his blue eyes disrupted the steady beat of her heart.

She turned quickly to face the front again and fought the rush of wild longing that swept through her. The cab of the truck suddenly seemed very cramped. She was conscious of his long, muscled thighs on the seat near hers and the sinewed strength of his arms beneath the sleeves of his shirt. It became difficult to think clearly in such close quarters and Charley tried to concentrate on the passing scenery.

"Where are we going?" she asked as she tried to recognize her surroundings.

"That's a surprise," Shad replied, deliberately mysterious.

"Tell me where you're taking me," she insisted. The game he was playing brought a reluctant smile to dimple the corners of her mouth.

"Somewhere out of this world," he said with a mocking grin and refused to tell her more than that.

Her curiosity was fully aroused as she sat back and watched the passing scenery. Her mind raced in an attempt to guess their ultimate destination. She made a lot of guesses and discarded them all, no nearer to unraveling the mystery than before. And Shad wouldn't help her.

CHAPTER FIVE

THE HIGHWAY swung along the foothills of the mountain range with the Snake River Plains spreading out flat on the other side. Charley was still in the dark about their destination until she saw the harsh, forbidding landscape ahead of them. Barren of plant life, it was a tortuous collection of volcanic rock and solidified lava.

"The Craters of the Moon, that's where we're going," she guessed accurately this time.

Shad chuckled and reminded her, "I told you it was someplace 'out of this world.'"

"That was a rotten clue and you know it." She poked her fist at his shoulder in a playful reprimand and laughed.

Slowing the truck, he turned into the entrance of the Craters of the Moon National Monument. The jagged rockscape flanked the road on either side of them. The colors varied from near black to a purplish gray. Shad stopped the truck in a small parking area along the side of the road.

"Come on," he said as he opened his own door. "Let's get out and walk."

Charley pushed her own door open and joined him by the front hood of the truck. Almost casually, he reached out and took hold of her hand to lead her onto the rough terrain. Charley didn't resist the warm grip of his hand as she followed him onto the uneven ground.

When the road disappeared behind them, an eerie silence seemed to descend, darkly lonely and mysterious. Shad paused in the center of this harsh, dangerous landscape and Charley lifted her face to the whispering breeze, pushing the hair back from her face and holding it there.

They were surrounded by cones and craters of volcanic rock. Long ago, massive underground explosions had created these weird formations and sent out the lava flows to create an island of rock crags in a land of grass and trees and earth. Its resemblance to photographs of the moon's surface was uncanny, so empty and lifeless.

Charley glanced over her shoulder at the mountain range on the horizon, needing the reassurance that this desolate landscape did not go on forever. When her gaze swung to Shad, his mouth curved in a smile of silent understanding.

"If a person ever wondered what it is like to walk on the moon, he'd have his answer here," he said.

"It's eerie, isn't it? So quiet and so lonely." She looked around, seeing nothing but more sharp rock formations.

"There's the moon." With a nod of his head he indicated the pale white orb in the daytime sky, its shadowy face barely discernible.

She moved closer to Shad, their arms brushing against each other as she lifted her gaze to the orbiting object. When he released her hand, she missed the warmth of his touch, but his arm curved itself around the back of her waist, replacing one sensation with another.

"It makes you feel isolated, doesn't it?" He turned his head to look at her and Charley felt the first tremor of desire quiver through her at how close they stood. "As if we are the only two people left, marooned here alone."

"Yes." It was a low answer, concealing the disturbance his remark provoked. It was a heady thought to be marooned with him—with no possibility that he could ever leave her.

"Have you ever wondered what it would be like to make love on the moon?" His question robbed her of speech. At the negative movement of her head, Shad turned slightly to more squarely face her. His dark head blocked out her view of the moon as he slowly gathered her into his arms, fitting her soft curves to his male shape. He rubbed his mouth across her forehead. "I have," he murmured against her skin, the warmth of his breath stimulating her nerve ends as he dragged his mouth to a temple. "It must be a very unique experience."

With soft kisses he closed her eyes to sentence her to a world of sensation. Her fingers curled into the hard muscles of his arms, clinging to him as she felt a strange weightlessness envelop her. While he explored the curve of her cheek and the corner of her lips, his hands roamed in exciting caresses over her shoulders and hips. He seemed to deliberately torment her with the promise of his kiss, but did not offer it.

The aching need that was building in her eventually forced a soft moan from her throat. In answer to her wordless plea, his hard lips covered her mouth with bruising possession. The circle of his arms tightened, crushing her breasts, taut with desire, against the unyielding wall of his chest. Yet not even this closeness brought satisfaction and she strained to cross the physical limits of their embrace, to become part of him.

His mouth broke away from hers, his breathing labored and heavy. She could feel the pounding of his heart, thudding as loudly as her own. His eyes were half-closed with the weight of desire as they ran over her face. He loosened his hold, bringing his hands up to curve them under the hair along her neck while Charley continued to lean against him, her legs too weak to stand without his support. His hands were restless with their caresses, his fingers exploring the curve of her jaw and the pulsing vein in her neck.

"Your body feels so good against mine," he murmured on a husky pitch and lowered one hand to cup it to her breast. It swelled beneath his touch. "I want to make love to you, Charley. You know that."

His statement pulled away the veil she'd been hiding behind and she could see clearly. The one thing she had been so determined to avoid had happened despite her better judgment. She had fallen irrevocably in love with him.

"It isn't fair," she protested in a faint sob. "I want you so much, Shad."

"Charley." Her name was a caress on his lips

100

as he brought them down hard on her own, stealing what little vestige of control she had left.

The embrace would have ended in her total surrender if it hadn't been for the clatter of a pair of feet on the rocky ground. The approach of the intruder stopped the kiss before it reached the point where they both would have been beyond hearing a bomb explode. Shad lifted his head at almost the same moment that the sound ceased. As his arms loosened to let Charley go his frown turned into a lazy smile.

"Who are you?" he asked, and Charley wondered how anyone could resist his smile. Still a little shaky, she turned to see who Shad was talking to. A little boy, no more than six years old, stood poised in the shadow of a volcanic cone. His rounded blue eyes were studying them uncertainly. "I'll bet I know who you are," Shad stated. "You're the man in the moon, aren't you?"

The little boy laughed and nodded vigorously that he was. Shad crouched down, sitting on his heels, to bring himself to eye level with the youngster.

"I've always wanted to meet the man in the moon," he remarked and looked him over. "I thought you'd be taller."

"I only look small," the boy said, his child's imagination liking this game. "I'm really bigger."

Charley could see that Shad was enjoying himself, too. He had a natural affinity with children, she realized. He would make a good father, she decided and caught herself wondering whether his son would inherit those blue eyes and black hair. She was treading in dangerous waters.

"I haven't had lunch yet and I'm starting to get hungry." Shad tipped his head at an inquiring angle. "I don't suppose you'd tell me where you keep the green cheese."

"The moon isn't made of cheese," the boy scoffed at him for believing such nonsense.

"It isn't?" Shad looked surprised.

At just about that same moment, a woman's voice called anxiously, "Billy! Billy, where are you?"

The boy turned with a reluctant sigh and answered, "Here, mom!"

A young woman in shorts and a knit top appeared a second later behind the cone where the boy waited. Her worried expression faded to exasperation as she found him unharmed. "You shouldn't go running away from your father and me like that. Don't you realize that you could have got lost?"

"But I didn't," he replied in a perfectly reasonable tone and turned to point to Shad and Charley. "They found me."

"You mean you aren't really the man in the moon?" Shad feigned a look of disappointment as he sent a brief smile at the boy's mother and straightened to his feet.

"No. I fooled you, didn't I?" the boy laughed.

"You certainly did," Shad agreed.

"I hope he wasn't a nuisance," the woman apologized and caught hold of her son's hand.

"Not at all," he assured her and sent a glance at Charley that contradicted his statement.

But the interruption had given Charley time to regain her senses. Shad's recognition of that fact flickered across his expression. Once they were alone, there wouldn't be a resumption of that embrace. The moment had passed when desire reigned supreme. Falling in love with him hadn't changed the reality that he would leave her someday. It had now become a question of how much she would be hurt, and not a question of whether she'd be hurt.

When the boy's father had joined his wife and son, Shad lightly took hold of Charley's hand. By mutual consent they retraced their route to the parking area where they'd left the truck.

After helping her into the cab, Shad walked around the hood to climb behind the wheel.

"Have you seen enough of the park?" He sent her a questioning glance as he started the engine.

"Yes." She made a show of glancing at her watch. "It's getting late. We'd better head back for the ranch before Gary starts wondering what happened to us."

Stepping on the accelerator, he turned onto the road and headed back toward the highway. "Do you want to stop somewhere for lunch?"

"I'm not hungry," she said, answering him with a negative shake of her head. "Are you?"

His gaze touched her, then swept to the jutting curves of her breasts. "Not for food," he replied and didn't need to add more. Her heart had already started fluttering against her ribs, guessing his hunger.

As they neared the highway she forced her attention to concentrate on the cross traffic. As soon as there was a break in the vehicles Shad accelerated onto the highway.

During the next twenty or so miles they didn't speak at all. Gradually her tension left Charley and she began to relax once again in Shad's company, her guard lowering. He seemed to sense the very moment it occurred, because he glanced over at her and smiled.

"Did you enjoy your excursion to the Craters of the Moon?" he asked. There was nothing in his tone to make Charley suspect she should read more into his question than what he had said.

"Very much." Which was true—in many ways, but she didn't let her thoughts dwell on that. Combing her fingers through her hair, she looked out the window and sighed contentedly.

"What was that for?" His glance was curious.

"I guess it was an expression of pride in my home state," she shrugged because she wasn't entirely sure what it had been. "Idaho has everything."

"Is that right?" His tone was faintly mocking.

"It's true," Charley insisted. "On the road toward Salmon, we have the Grand Canyon in miniature. East of here, there are sand dunes. And Shoshone Falls outside of Twin Falls, Idaho. The water there falls farther than the waters at Niagara Falls. There's the Snake River Canyon and the Salmon 'River of No Return.' I could go on and on."

"I noticed," he chuckled in a way that gently teased her.

"Well, it does have everything." She laughed at her own enthusiasm.

"I wouldn't dream of arguing with you," he replied and reached out to link his fingers with hers. A warm tingle of pleasure ran up her arm at his gesture of affection and closeness. "Is there a reason why there has to be so much room on the seat between us?" Shad asked with a coaxing smile.

Charley hesitated but the temptation to be close to him was too strong to resist. Besides, as long as he was driving, it seemed relatively safe. And there wouldn't be many chances to be near him.

"I suppose not," she admitted and shifted over to sit beside him.

Unlinking their hands, he put his arm around her so that she was snuggling in the crook of his shoulder with his hand on her waist. It was a natural, comfortable position with the warmth of his body pressed alongside hers.

"What's the longest you've ever stayed in one place?" Charley wondered aloud.

"Two years," he replied without any hesitation.

"Haven't you ever considered settling

down?'' There was a wistful quality to her question as she indulged herself in the ridiculous dream that she might be the one to persuade him to put down roots.

"Yes," Shad admitted. "I spent two years trying. That was five years ago when I was twenty-nine. I decided it was time I stayed in one place and build myself a home. So I bought a small ranch over on the Idaho side of the Bitterroot Mountains."

"You did?" Charley was surprised by his answer.

"Yes." And he went on to explain, "In the beginning, it was a challenge to fix the place up and bring the ranch up to its potential. I worked day and night at it, running new fence during the daytime and repairing the buildings at night."

"If you liked it, why didn't you stay?" She was confused.

"It's like having a new toy. When you first get it, you don't want to play with anything else. Later on, the newness wears off and you become bored with it. That's what happened to me with the ranch. Once it was running smoothly and on the verge of showing a profit, the old urge to travel came back. There wasn't anything to keep me there."

"So you sold it and moved on," Charley concluded, depression settling onto her shoulders.

"I moved on but I didn't sell it," Shad corrected her on that point. "A widower and his son manage it for me on a share basis. I have a small but steady income from it, which allows me to do pretty much what I please. It's a place I can go to when I'm too old to travel."

"Have you ever been back to the ranch since you left it?" she asked.

"No. I was headed there when you walked into that café that day," he said with a downward glance that sparkled over her face. "I can't say for sure what made me change my plans that morning. I didn't need the money then so I guess it was the idea of having a honey-haired boss." His gaze made one sweep of the highway in front of them before Shad turned and bent his head to steal a kiss.

The sudden possession of his mouth caught her off guard. It took her a full second to recover her scattered wits. Her heart continued to trip over itself in an effort to find its normal rhythm.

"You'd better pay attention to your driving," Charley attempted to sound stern, but her voice was on the breathless side.

Laughter came from deep within his chest as

his arm tightened around her, hugging her closer still. "You're a helluva woman, Charley. I've never met anybody like you. And *that* isn't a line," he informed her with underlining emphasis.

Charley fell silent, a faint smile curving her mouth as she savored his compliment and basked in the warmth of its afterglow. They passed through Ketchum and the turnoff to the skiing community of Sun Valley. The road to the Collins's ranch was not many miles away.

Eventually her thoughts returned to the one fact that she could never ignore for long. She found she had to ask him, "Why do you always have to move on, Shad?"

"I don't know." He seemed to consider her question with all the seriousness with which she asked it. "Maybe I was born with a wanderlust in my soul. When I was younger, I thought I would come to a place, look around and say to myself, 'This is it. This is where I'm going to stay.' But it doesn't happen like that. After I've been in new territory for a while, I start looking around and wondering what's across the river or over the next hill. It's taken me a while, but I've finally learned that there will always be one more river to cross."

His answer made it very clear to Charley that

she was foolish to hope she could ever change him. She couldn't change herself. As much as she loved him she would never truly be happy traveling around the country. She would always be longing for a place to call home. It didn't seem fair. She felt the sting of tears burning her eyes and blinked to keep them at bay.

When they finally reached the ranch lane, Shad needed both hands on the steering wheel to make the sharp turn. As he removed his arm from around her Charley shifted to her own side of the truck. His frowning glance took note of the movement and the whiteness of her face.

"Why have you become so silent again?" he demanded after several seconds had passed. "Is something wrong?"

"No. I was just trying to decide how I was going to keep from crying when you leave." The truth came out on a note of forced lightness.

It silenced him for a minute. "Charley, you do tempt me to stay." The very steadiness of his voice revealed that he meant what he had said.

She laughed with a tinge of bitterness as the truck slowed down to enter the ranch yard. "Let's be honest, Shad. All I do is 'tempt' you, but you'll leave just the same."

The instant the truck stopped she reached for the door handle and climbed out of the cab. A door slammed behind her as she started for the house. Shad caught up with her before she reached the porch steps, his hand gripping her arm to turn her around.

"Charley—" He started to speak but she didn't want to listen to what he had to say.

"Just leave me alone, Shad. Don't hurt me any more than you have already." She stood rigidly before him, warily defiant. "You said it yourself—you're no good for me." She threw his own words back at him and he recoiled from their sting, letting her go.

Her legs were shaking as she climbed the steps and crossed the porch to the front door. She wanted to run, but she managed to make a dignified retreat. Gary was just inside the door, leaning on his crutches. He knew her too well not to read what was written on her face.

"I heard the truck drive in.... Oh, Charley," he groaned in sympathy. "What have you done?"

"Made a fool of myself as usual. What do you think?" She tried to joke aside the hurt and futile longing in her expression.

"If you had to fall for somebody, why couldn't it have been Weatherby? I grant you he'll never win any prize in a Mr. America contest but at least he would have caught you when

111

you fell," Gary muttered sadly. "You knew right from the beginning that he was a drifter."

"I knew—and I tried not to care," she admitted, hanging her head in acknowledgement of failure. "But it didn't change anything."

Gary sighed, "Maybe I should have a talk with Russell."

"No. Just let it be," she urged her brother not to interfere. "There isn't anything you can do to help me. I have to handle this alone, the same way you did," she nodded, alluding to his broken engagement.

"It hurts like hell, Charley," he commiserated with a look of pain.

"Don't I know." Her short laugh was brittle. She turned away, feeling her composure start to crumble. "I have a headache. I think I'll go upstairs and lie down for a while."

"Is there anything I can bring you?" her brother offered.

"No." She hurried to the steps before she started crying.

THERE WERE TIMES when Charley wondered if she would survive the next ten days. Shad stayed clear of her and she could never seem to make up her mind whether she was happy or sad about that. He found a lot of reasons to ride away from the ranch during the day to check on the cattle or repair fences. Mealtimes were stilted affairs with no one saying very much. The evenings Shad either spent in his room or cleaning the tack in the barn or overhauling some piece of machinery.

She rarely saw him smile anymore. He remained aloof whenever she was around, always very brisk and businesslike. Yet this constant avoidance of the issue only intensified the strain they were all under.

On Saturday, Shad came to the house, quitting work early. He did no more than nod in Charley's direction before climbing the stairs to his room. When she heard the shower running in the upstairs bathroom, she went into the kitchen to peel the potatoes for their evening meal.

Twenty minutes later she heard him coming down the stairs—whistling! The happy sound pivoted her around. She was facing the doorway when Shad walked through it. Freshly shaved with his black hair glistening, he was wearing a snow-white shirt and a leather vest. A pair of dark pants snugly fit his slim hips.

"Don't bother to fix any supper for me tonight. I won't be here," he said.

"Where are you going?" She could have bitten off her tongue for asking such a nosy question. It really wasn't any business of hers what he did with his evenings, but it was too late. It had already been asked.

His mouth twisted into a kind of wry grin. "What does a cowboy usually do on a Saturday night? He has himself a steak dinner, romances the ladies, and gets drunk." Gary entered the kitchen in time to hear his answer and Shad turned to look at him. "What about it, Gary? Do you want to go with me?"

"You'll probably need me to carry you home," he said dryly and shook his head in refusal, "but I think I'll pass on the invitation and wait until I have two sound legs before going out on the town."

"Have it your way," Shad shrugged indifferently. "See you later."

Charley turned to face the sink as he walked out the back door. From the window above the sink, she could see him cross the yard to the old pickup. There was a lump in her throat as she watched him drive out of the yard.

"Charley." Her brother spoke her name softly.

"I'm all right," she insisted, but was careful not to look at him. "It really doesn't make much difference, does it? When he leaves here,

114

I'll be imagining him with some other woman so I might as well get used to it now."

"I wish you wouldn't be so hard on yourself," Gary complained.

"It would be worse if I pretended he was going to stay," she reminded him.

CHAPTER SIX

AFTER SUPPER Gary helped her clear the table and do the dishes, which was practically unheard-of coming from him. Propping himself against the sink, with the crutches under his arms for support, he washed the dishes while Charley dried them and put them away.

"How about a game of checkers?" he suggested when they were finished.

"I'm not really in the mood—" she started to refuse, then realized he was trying to be thoughtful and keep her mind away from Shad and what he might be doing. She smiled quickly. "All right, why not?"

The first two games were close, although Gary won them both, but he was the better checker player, too. On the third, her concentration faltered and it was barely a contest. Her gaze kept straying to the kitchen wall clock as the evening crept by. Charley lost the fourth and fifth games, too.

When the sixth showed signs of turning into a rout, her brother grumbled, "I can't believe that anyone I taught to play checkers could play the game so badly."

"I'm sorry," she sighed. "I wasn't paying attention." Her glance darted to the wall clock.

"It's twenty-five minutes to ten," Gary said dryly. "The last time you looked it was twenty-seven minutes to ten."

"I'm sorry." She felt guilty because he was trying so hard to keep her entertained.

"And stop saying you're sorry." He flashed her an impatient look.

"I'm—" She had been on the verge of saying it again and caught herself just in time. They looked at each other and laughed, breaking the invisible tension in the air. "It's no use, Gary," Charley sighed. "I might as well admit defeat now. I can't concentrate."

"It's a losing battle, isn't it?" He dumped the checkers into their box, calling it quits.

"Yes, but it was a nice thought," she said as she pushed her chair away from the kitchen table.

"What are you going to do?" He put the lid on the box and handed it to her so she could put it away in the cupboard.

"I think I'll take a long soak in the tub—and hopefully scrub that man out from under my skin," Charley joked with a self-mocking smile.

"Good luck." Gary sounded suitably doubtful of her success. As he started to pull himself upright with his crutches he winced and turned white with pain, sitting back down again.

"What's wrong?" she frowned with instant concern.

"Nothing," he insisted. "I've just been sitting in one position too long. It'll pass." He tried to stand up again and Charley could see that it hurt him but he finally managed to get upright.

"Are you sure you don't want one of those pain pills the doctor prescribed for you?" she suggested.

"No, it'll go away." But his jaw was clenched against the discomfort as he bit down hard.

"You won't make it easy on yourself, will you?" she chided him. "You have to tough it out."

His gaze flashed her a challenge. "Look who's talking." He reminded Charley of her own harshly realistic outlook.

"All right, I'll stop throwing stones," she promised and started toward the stairwell in the living room. "If you need anything, call me."

"I will," he promised.

In the second-floor bathroom, she turned on the water faucets in the tub and adjusted the water temperature until it was comfortably hot. She dumped in some bubble bath. On impulse she added an extra splash, giving in to a whim of self-indulgence. There had been enough misery in her life of late and she decided she deserved a little pampering.

While the tub was filling with water she went into her bedroom to undress and get her cotton bathrobe. When she returned, the bathtub was mounded with bubbles. Turning off the faucets, Charley piled her hair on top of her head, secured it with a comb, and climbed into the tub to stretch out the full length of it, resting her head on the curved porcelain back. She closed her eyes and let the fragrant water act as a balm to soothe her inner aches.

After she had been in the tub barely ten minutes, she heard the thump of Gary's crutches in the living room below. The sound was followed by the opening of the stairwell door.

"Charley!" He called up to her and she

frowned at the interruption of her quiet bath. "Where are those pain pills from the doctor?"

She opened her eyes in surprise. His leg must really be bothering him for Gary to give in and ask for the pills. "They're in the medicine cabinet." She shouted the answer, and heard him thump away.

In a few minutes he was back. "Charley!"

"What?"

"I can't find them! What kind of bottle are they in?" His patience seemed to be running thin.

"It's brown!" She called down and waited as he thumped off again.

This time he wasn't gone as long and his voice was decidedly more irritable when he called, "There are three bottles in the medicine cabinet that are brown! How am I supposed to tell them apart?"

Charley sighed in mild exasperation. "I'll get them!"

Climbing out of the tub, she grabbed a towel and blotted the excess moisture from her body. Her robe was hanging on the door hook. She slipped into it, tugging the cotton material over her damp skin and buttoning it as she hurried out of the bathroom to the staircase.

Once she was downstairs, Gary protested,

"You could have told me what to look for. You didn't have to come down."

"Now you tell me," she retorted. Then she saw how white his face was beneath the tan and added in a gentler tone, "I don't mind. It's better than wondering if you took a pill from the wrong bottle."

With Gary following her, she went to the medicine cabinet in the downstairs bathroom and took out the brown bottle containing his medication. She didn't bother to point out to him that neither of the other two brown bottles contained pills. One was iodine and the other held cotton balls. She gave him the prescribed dosage and a glass of water to wash them down.

"I'll help you into bed," Charley volunteered.

"My leg hurts too much to lie down," he refused her suggestion with a frowning shake of his head.

"Listen, when those pills start to work, you'll be knocked out. And I can't get you into bed by myself so you're going there now," she ordered and Gary gave in.

By the time she tucked the covers around him, he was already beginning to feel the effects. She turned off the light as she left the room and went back upstairs to the bath she'd left. The bubbles had all dissolved and the water was barely tepid. Most of her enthusiasm for a long, luxurious bath had evaporated, too. She pulled the plug to let the water run down the drain. As it gurgled noisily, she scrubbed away the soap scum from the sides of the porcelain tub. Once the bathwater was gone, she ran cold water out of the faucets to give the tub one final rinse.

Just as she finished, Charley thought she heard a noise downstairs. She stopped to listen, thinking maybe Gary was calling for her but there was only silence. Yet she was positive she'd heard something, so she went downstairs to check.

She tiptoed quietly into her brother's room. The outside yard light cast its beam through the window by his bed. Gary was sleeping soundly, his chest rising and falling in a slow, steady rhythm beneath the cover of the blankets. Reassured that he was all right, Charley slipped out of the room.

A flash of white in the living room caught her eye a split second before a low voice said, "Charley?"

She smothered her startled cry of alarm with her hand as Shad materialized from the shadows. Her hand slipped down to cover her rapidly beating heart.

"You startled me," she accused.

"Sorry. I didn't mean to," he apologized and glanced beyond her to the bedroom door. "Is Gary all right?"

"Yes. His leg was bothering him earlier and he took a couple of pain pills. I was just checking on him to make sure he was okay," she explained. The initial surprise of his sudden appearance in the house had gone. In its place was the sharp memory of where he'd been. "What are you doing back so soon?" Charley challenged in an icy voice. "I thought you were going to stay out until all hours of the morning."

"I was." His voice was low, unruffled by her tone.

It was difficult to see his face in the shadowy dimness of the room. There weren't any lights on downstairs. What light there was came from the stairwell or the yard light outside. Yet Charley could feel the disturbing intensity of his gaze.

"Then what are you doing here?" Forced anger was her defense against him.

"After I had my steak dinner, I went to a bar. There was this drunk there...." His voice took on a different quality, gentle, almost caressing. "He kept singing 'Charley is my darling.' And I started wondering what I was doing in that bar when my Charley was here.''

Her heart cried out for him, loving him all the more for saying such beautiful words, but it hurt, too. Charley turned her head away, closing her eyes tightly.

"Don't say such things, Shad." She pleaded with him not to hurt her anymore.

"Why not?" he countered. "It's what I feel.

She tried to take the potency from his words by accusing, "You've been drinking."

"Yes, I've been drinking," he admitted. As she started to walk away from him, he caught her wrist and pulled her around. She was in his arms before she had a chance to resist. "But I'm not drunk."

"Let me go, Shad." She tried to twist out of his arms but they tightened around her, holding her fast. The warmth of his hands burned through the thin material of her robe, setting her flesh afire.

"My God!" He issued the stunned exclamation under his breath as he became suddenly motionless. An exploring hand moved over her hip. "You don't have anything on under this."

Aware of the imprint his body was making on hers, her own senses echoed the aroused note in his voice. Yet she tried to resist it.

"Shad, don't," she protested.

But he merely groaned and rubbed his shaven cheek against hers, brushing her ear with his mouth. "It's no use, Charley. I've tried to stay away from you, but I can't. Let's forget about tomorrow. We have today. Better yet, we have tonight."

His mouth rocked over her lips, persuading and cajoling, sensually chewing on her lower lip until she was reeling. Restless male hands wandered the length of her spine, arousing and loving the feel of her. She was helpless against this loving attack.

"We can't go on like this, denying ourselves," Shad muttered thickly as her lips grazed along his jaw. "It's tearing us both apart. Isn't it?"

"Yes." The aching admission was torn from her throat, the ability to reason lost.

It was the answer he had been waiting for as he swept her off her feet and into his arms. Her hands circled his neck while her mouth investigated the strong column of his throat, savoring the taste of him. He carried her to the couch and lowered her to the cushions while he sat on the edge facing her.

He leaned down to cover her parted lips with his mouth, his hard tongue probing behind the white barrier of her teeth to have the satisfaction of total possession. Raw desire licked through her veins, a spreading fire that left none of her body untouched. His large hands deftly loosened the buttons of her robe and pushed the material aside to expose her flesh to his tactile explorations.

Jealous of the liberties he enjoyed, her fingers tugged at the buttons of his shirt. When the last one was unfastened, Shad aided her by pulling his shirt free of his waistband. She moaned softly as she felt the heat of his flesh beneath her hands. Her fingers ran eagerly over his flexed and rippling muscles, excited and stimulated by this freedom to touch and caress.

Forsaking the passion of her lips, his mouth began a downward path. Delighted quivers erupted through her skin as he explored the sensitive cord in her neck and drank from the hollow of her throat. Her fingernails dug into his flesh when his mouth grazed along the slope of her breast, its point hardening with desire, eventually luring his attention to it. Charley shuddered with uninhibited longing under the arousing manipulation of his tongue.

When she was weak with need, he returned to bruise her lips with his kisses. "Tell me you want me, Charley," he urged. "I've been haunted by your voice saying those words. I want to hear them again.''

"I want you, Shad," she whispered against his skin. "More than that, I love you."

"I want you more than I've ever wanted any other woman in my life," he told her roughly.

"I want you to stay with me tonight, Shad," Charley murmured. "Tonight and tomorrow night and every night of my life. I don't want you to leave me."

"You know I can't promise that, Charley," he muttered thickly, rubbing his mouth over her cheek.

She knew. Her arms curved more tightly around him, fusing the warmth of his bare flesh against her own. "Hold me," she whispered. "Don't ever let me go." Her eyes were tightly closed, but a tear squeezed its way through her lashes. It was followed by more until Shad tasted the salty moisture on her skin.

"Don't cry, Charley." The roughness of his calloused hand was on her cheek, wiping them away. "For God's sake, don't cry." His voice held no anger, only a kind of anguished regret.

"I can't help it." She honestly tried to check the flow of tears but it was unstoppable.

With a heavy sigh he eased his weight from her and sat up. She blinked and felt the touch of his hands as he folded the front of her robe shut. Then he was leaning his elbows on his knees and raking his fingers through his hair to rub the back of his neck. Charley sat up, a hand unconsciously holding the front of her robe. She touched his shoulder, tentative, uncertain.

"No, Charley," he said, then turned his head to look at her. A dark, troubled light was in his eyes. "I swear to God I never meant to hurt you."

"I know," she murmured gently and a little sadly. "It isn't your fault. You didn't ask me to fall in love with you. Maybe if you had, I'd be able to hate you, but I don't."

She swung her feet to the floor and slowly walked to the stairs, leaving Shad sitting there alone on the couch. It was almost an hour later before she heard him come upstairs. He paused at the top of the stairs and Charley held her breath. Finally the door to his bedroom opened and closed. The tears started again.

SLEEP became something that eluded Charley. The hours that she didn't spend staring at the ceiling, she tossed and turned fitfully. By Wednesday morning the lack of rest began to paint faint shadows below her eyes. They didn't go unnoticed by her brother.

"Aren't you feeling well, Charley?" he asked at the breakfast table Wednesday morning, eyeing her critically.

"I'm fine," she insisted.

"Well, you don't look so good," he concluded bluntly.

"Thanks," she snapped and paled under Shad's scrutiny.

Gary noticed the exchange and his eyes narrowed suspiciously, but he made no comment. Charley knew that her brother had probably guessed the cause for her sleeplessness, but there was nothing he could do about it.

When she crawled into bed that night, she expected it to be a repeat of the previous nights. She listened for the longest time, waiting for the sound of Shad's footsteps on the stairs. She dozed off without hearing, then awakened later and strained to hear sounds of him sleeping in the other bedroom. Finally fatigue overtook her and she fell into a heavy sleep.

The buzz of the alarm clock was insistent, dragging open her eyelids despite her attempt to ignore it. She climbed wearily from the bed, irritated that the one time she had managed to sleep, she had been forced to waken. She dressed in her usual garb of blue jeans and blouse and left the bedroom in a kind of daze.

At the door to the bathroom, her glance was attracted to Shad's bedroom. The door was shut. She didn't know whether he was still sleeping or was already downstairs. Not that it mattered, she told herself and entered the bathroom. With her face washed and her teeth brushed, she lost some of that drugged feeling.

At the bottom of the stairs, Charley was shocked to find Shad sleeping on the couch in the living room. Too tall for it, he was sprawled over the length of the cushions with his feet poking over the end of the armrest. From somewhere, he'd gotten a blanket. It was loosely draped over him. She couldn't imagine what he was doing sleeping on the couch. She walked over to waken him.

Her hand touched his shoulder and he stirred, frowning in his sleep. The second time Charley gripped his shoulder more firmly and combined the action with the use of his name. "Shad. Shad. It's time to get up."

With a flex of his shoulder, he shrugged away her hand but he opened his eyes. They focused slowly on Charley's face as she stood half-leaning over him. His mouth tiredly curved into one of his slow smiles.

"Good morning." His voice was husky with sleep, its drawl thicker.

"Good morning," she returned the greeting and started to ask him what he was doing on the couch, but his hand reached out to snare one of hers and pull her onto the cushion beside him.

"Don't I get more of a greeting than that?" Shad mocked and hooked his hand behind her neck to force her head down.

Charley stopped needing direction when she neared his mouth. Her lips settled into it naturally and moved in response to his sampling kiss. She wasn't breathing quite normally when she finally straightened. He started to shift his position and winced from a cramped muscle. The discomfort made him take note of his "bed." He seemed to register vague surprise when he found himself on the couch.

"Why are you sleeping here?" Charley finally asked her question.

"The mood I was in last night, if I had gone upstairs, I would have ended up sleeping in your bed." There was rough impatience in his expression as his hands settled onto the soft flesh of her upper arms and began rubbing them absently.

"Oh, Shad." She trembled with the quick onrush of desire.

"Yes, you should say, 'Oh, Shad.' I don't think you know what you're doing to me," he muttered. "At this rate, I'm going to be sleeping in the barn next, just to keep my hands off you."

Neither of them heard the muffled thud of Gary's crutches. They were too engrossed in each other to pay attention to anything else. Neither did they see him enter the living room and stop to stare at them.

"What's going on here?" he frowned suspiciously, puzzled to see Shad using the couch for a bed.

Charley turned swiftly to face her brother but Shad was slow to let his hands slide from her arms, showing no signs of guilt.

"I was just waking up Shad," Charley explained, aware that her cheeks felt warm.

"What are you doing sleeping on the couch?" Gary ignored her to question Shad.

"All things considered—" his glance briefly touched Charley to indicate what things were considered "—it seemed the proper place to sleep last night."

Gary came farther into the room, his gaze not leaving Shad. "Are you getting any ideas about fooling around with my sister?" he demanded.

"The ideas are there," Shad admitted, "but so far my conscience has won. It's becoming more of a struggle, though."

132

Charley couldn't handle this conversation and quickly found an excuse to leave before it went any further. "I'd better start breakfast," she said and rose quickly to disappear into the kitchen. The conversation between Shad and her brother didn't end with her departure. She listened to what was said from the kitchen, biting her lip in nervous anxiety.

"I don't want to see Charley get hurt," Gary stated.

"If I didn't feel the same way, I would have been sleeping upstairs instead of down here," Shad replied with a trace of impatience.

"The kindest thing you could do is leave her alone—" Her brother began to issue advice but Shad interrupted him before he had finished.

"Don't preach to me, Gary," he warned in an angry voice.

"I think you're forgetting that you are paid to work for me," Gary countered, reacting to the angry tone.

"You're right. There are a lot of things I've been forgetting lately," Shad declared in an ominous tone. "Like—what the hell am I still doing here!"

Charley heard heavy strides cross the room and climb the stairs. It was several seconds before Gary started for the kitchen where she waited. His expression was grim when he entered.

"Why did you say those things to him?" She shook her head wearily.

"You are my sister. What did you expect me to do?" he argued.

"Shad isn't leaving, is he?" Although her voice was calm, there was fear in her eyes.

"I don't think so, not now at any rate," Gary replied and looked at her sadly. "Charley, you know he's going to leave sooner or later."

"Yes," she admitted. "But I don't want him to go now. Not yet."

THE WOODEN POSTS rumbled in the back end of the pickup truck as Charley drove across the pasture meadow to where Shad was running a new section of fence near the timberline. This last load of posts would take him to the end.

When he saw her coming he swung the post-hole digger aside, letting it fall to the ground near the partially dug hole. With slow energy-conserving strides, he walked to where she had stopped the truck. Charley was already out of the cab and lowering the tailgate.

As she grabbed for a fence post to drag it out of the truck Shad ordered crisply, "Don't be lifting those. I'll unload the posts."

"I can manage," she insisted. "I've done it before."

When she continued to pull the end of the post out of the truck bed, his gloved hand bit into her arm. "I said leave it! I don't care what you've done before. As long as I'm here, I'll do the unloading!"

She had never seen that angry blaze in his eyes before or the uncompromising set of his features. He was almost a stranger to her. Charley let go of the post and Shad released her arm. She moved stiffly to one side.

"All right, I won't help, but you don't have to bite my head off!" she retorted.

He paused and leaned his hands on the tailgate, staring at the ground. When he lifted his head to look at her, much of the anger was gone but his expression was still tautly controlled.

"I'm not angry with you, Charley," he explained. "I'm angry with myself for letting this situation develop."

"You couldn't help it," she said, because it wasn't solely his doing.

"Maybe not, but it doesn't matter." He straightened, eyeing her steadily. "I can't ask a woman to share the kind of life I lead. It wouldn't be fair to her. It wouldn't work."

Charley didn't understand why he was bringing the subject up, unless—"Do you want me to go with you when you leave?"

"No." His answer was definite. "I'm telling you why I don't want you to come with me when I go."

He reached for a post and began sliding it out of the truck and onto the ground. Charley stood quietly beside the truck, letting no expression show on her face as she watched him. When he had finished unloading the fence posts he glanced at her briefly.

"I'll see you at lunch," he said.

With a nod, she turned and walked to the cab, climbing in the driver's side. There was a big emptiness inside her as she drove away.

CHAPTER SEVEN

IT WAS NEARLY NOON on Monday before Charley drove the truck into the ranch yard after taking Gary to town to keep his doctor's appointment. The doctor had decided to remove the cast a week early so her brother was in a buoyant mood.

As she slowed the truck to a stop in front of the house she noticed Shad's saddle and gear sitting on the porch. Alarm shivered through her. Gary said something to her but she didn't hear him as she bolted from the truck and raced up the porch steps into the house.

Inside the living room, she stopped to face Shad. He was carrying his duffel bag. Her heart was pounding wildly in her ears as she stared at him for several long seconds, unable to speak.

Finally she said, "Where are you going?"

"Isn't it obvious? I'm leaving," he stated flatly. "You knew the day would come when I'd move on."

"You were going without saying a word. You were just going to be gone when we came back," she accused in disbelief.

"It seemed the easiest way." His jaw was hard, all expression held tightly in check.

"But to go without even telling me goodbye." She didn't understand how he could do that.

"You once told me that you were trying to decide how you were going to keep from crying when I left. At least give me credit for trying to spare you that," Shad stated.

"Don't go," Charley protested, trying hard not to plead with him.

"There's nothing you can say that will make me change my mind," he said firmly. "I should have left before now. I've waited too long as it is."

The screen door slammed as Gary walked in.

"Hello, Shad." His high spirits told Charley that he hadn't noticed any special significance in Shad's gear sitting outside. "As you can see, I've thrown away my crutches for a cane." Gary waggled it in the air. "They took the cast off today. Of course, Charley forgot to bring me some regular trousers so I had to walk out of the doctor's office with my pant leg cut off and my hairy white leg showing, but I feel ten pounds lighter.'' He paused, his glance lighting on the bag in Shad's hand. ''Are you going somewhere?''

''I'm leaving,'' Shad repeated himself to her brother.

''Without letting us know?'' Gary echoed her own words.

''Yes, and I've been all through that with your sister,'' he replied, irritated.

''This is very sudden.'' Gary frowned and glanced at Charley, trying to see by her expression if she'd known about this beforehand.

''You could have at least had the decency to give us a week's notice,'' Charley declared. ''We would have had a chance to find someone to take your place. Gary has his cast off but it'll be a couple of weeks before he gets the strength back in his leg.''

''That's true,'' Gary backed her up. ''You are leaving us in the lurch. Charley can't possibly do all the work by herself and I'm not going to be that much help to her for a while yet.''

Shad's mouth became compressed in a taut line as his gaze slashed from one to the other. ''All right,'' he gave in reluctantly, suppressing his anger. "One week. I'm giving you one week's notice from this morning. If you haven't found someone to take my place by then, I'm leaving anyway."

"Agreed," Charley said.

When he pivoted away and started up the stairs to put his bag away, Gary glanced at her. "What did you gain out of that, Charley?"

"Time," she said quietly. "Time to hire another man. That's all."

CHARLEY NOTICED that Shad didn't bother to unpack his duffel bag. His saddle and gear were stowed in the old pickup truck. When the time came, he would be gone in a matter of minutes. And that time wasn't far off.

The back door to the kitchen opened and Charley glanced over her shoulder to see Shad enter the house. Her initial rush of pleasure at seeing him faded quickly and she turned back to the stove to stir the tomato sauce in the pan.

"Lunch will be ready in a few minutes," she told him, trying not to let her mind make the countdown—only five more days, five more lunches to share.

"Have you found anyone to take over for me yet?" He came to stand beside her, his nearness disturbing her as always.

"No."

"Have you even made any inquiries yet?" Shad demanded with barely concealed impatience.

"I've been too busy," Charley replied.

He sighed heavily in disgust. "What are you trying to prove?"

"Nothing," she insisted.

"I meant what I said, Charley. I'm not staying one hour longer than my week's notice," he reminded her tersely.

"I'm aware of that," she murmured and closed her eyes as he walked away to wash up for the noon meal.

THE FOLLOWING AFTERNOON Charley was just leaving the house to help her brother with the evening chores when Shad drove up in his old pickup and stopped in front of the house. He walked right past her without saying a word and went into the house. Something about his purposeful stride started the dread to gnaw at her stomach. She waited on the porch. Within minutes he came out of the house with his duffel bag.

"What are you doing?" She stared at him, not quite accepting the evidence with her own eyes.

"This time I am leaving," he said and shouldered his way by her to descend the porch steps.

"But you can't," she protested. "You gave us a week's notice. There's still four more days left."

Opening the cab door, he heaved the duffel bag inside and turned to look at her. "Since you didn't seem to be in any great hurry to find someone to replace me, I took the matter into my own hands."

"What have you done?" There was little force behind her demand.

"I went to see your boyfriend this afternoon, Chuck Weatherby," Shad replied.

"He isn't my boyfriend," she denied even though it was hardly important at this moment.

"I explained to him that I had to leave," Shad went on as if she hadn't interrupted him. "I asked him if he could spare one of his men to help you out for a couple of weeks until Gary can manage on his own."

"You didn't," Charley breathed.

"I did," he stated. "A man will be over first thing in the morning. I'm leaving now."

But as he turned to slide behind the wheel, Gary rounded the front of the truck, leaning heavily on his cane. The truck had blocked him from view when he crossed the ranch yard from the barns. He sized the situation up instantly.

"Are you leaving, Shad?" he asked for confirmation.

"Yes. Chuck Weatherby is sending over one of his men in the morning." His chin was thrust forward at a challenging angle, prepared to argue the issue of his leaving.

But Gary had no intention of arguing. Instead he offered Shad his hand. "Thanks for all you've done. We couldn't have managed without you."

His grim expression relented slightly, allowing a smile to twitch the corners of his mouth as he shook hands with her brother. "Take care."

"Don't go!" Charley flew down the porch steps and stopped abruptly before she reached Shad.

"Nothing is going to stop me this time, Charley. Not even you." His eyes were hard points of blue steel, unwavering.

"You don't have to leave this minute." She was hurt and a little angry as she faced him defiantly. "You can at least stay long enough to hear what I have to say."

"It has all been said." He shook his head grimly. "Nothing has changed."

"I know I can't persuade you to change your

mind, but you can at least hear me out!'' she flared.

"All right," Shad agreed, his mouth thinning. "Say what it is that's on your mind and get it over with."

"You know I don't want you to leave but I'm not going to beg you to stay. So you don't need to worry that I'm going to cause an unpleasant scene." Her voice contained the hoarseness of pain, but it remained steady and forceful. "I just want you to know that I've figured out a few things about you, Shad Russell."

"Such as?" His attitude was one of almost cynical indulgence. Charley was stung by the way he appeared to be enduring these last few minutes with her.

"Such as the reasons why you never stay in one place." Her throat muscles were so tight she felt as if she was being strangled. "It isn't because you have this itch to roam, like you pretend."

"Is that right?" He openly mocked her.

"Yes, that's right. Because if you stayed in one place, you might start to care for someone. And when you care for someone, you have to make a commitment to them. You don't want to see what's on the other side of the hill. No, you're afraid of being responsible for someone other than yourself. You don't know how to be a friend, so you won't take a chance and find out!"

"Are you finished?" He didn't appear to have heard a single word she'd said. She was almost crying with frustration.

"Not quite!" Her voice was raw and husky. "I love you. And if you had an ounce of sense, you'd stay right here and marry me. But you don't so you're going to do what you always do—move on down the road." She paused to take a breath. "There's just one more thing I want to say."

"That's encouraging," Shad murmured dryly.

"If you leave now, I won't be waiting for you if you decide to come back!" Her voice was breaking, her control cracking. "I mean it, I won't wait. I'm not going to pine my life away for a foolhearted man like you, Shad Russell!"

"Are you finished *now*?" he asked.

"Yes!" Charley choked on a sob and swallowed it before it escaped to humiliate her. Her hands were clenched into tight fists at her side while she stood tall and unmoving before him.

There wasn't a word offered in farewell as Shad turned and climbed in behind the wheel of the pickup. His gaze didn't stray to her when the motor grumbled to life. There wasn't a look or a wave as the truck pulled away from the house.

"I won't wait for you, Shad!" Charley cried again. Gary limped over to put an arm around her shoulders in silent comfort. Silent sobs began to shake her shoulders as Shad circled the ranch yard and headed down the lane to the highway. "The stupid fool! Hasn't he ever seen any movies? Doesn't he know that he's supposed to turn right around and come back to me?" She sobbed in a crazy kind of anger.

Seconds later the truck disappeared from sight. Soon she couldn't even hear the sound of its motor. Burying her face in her hands, she started crying. Gary turned her into his arms, hugging her close while his chin rubbed the top of her head.

"I'm sorry, Charley," he murmured.

She leaned on him, unable to stop the flood of tears. Sobs racked her shoulders, tearing her apart. There was no relief from the pain inside.

"Come on, Charley. There's no point in standing out here," Gary urged. "Let's go in the house."

She let herself be turned toward the porch, leaning heavily on the support of his arm. Too blinded by tears to see where she was going, she let Gary lead her. She stumbled up the steps and across the porch floor to the door, the retching sobs continuing to tear at her chest. Inside the house he guided her to the sofa and sat down with her.

"That's enough, Charley." Her brother betrayed his inability to handle her tears. "Crying isn't going to help. If you keep this up, you're going to make yourself sick."

Pulling a handkerchief from his pocket, he tried to dam the flow of tears by awkwardly dabbing at her eyes. In self-defense, Charley took the hankie from him and honestly tried to stop crying. The sobbing was reduced to painful, hiccuping breaths.

"That's better." There was relief in his voice.

But it wasn't, not really. It was all on the inside now, all the pain and the heartache. She sat up, sniffling loudly, and pressed her lips tightly together to stop her chin from quivering. Her fingers twisted into the handkerchief, wadding it into a tight ball. Then she was noisily blowing her nose and sniffling some more.

"Damn him!" She swore at Shad, her voice taut and choked with pain.

"Now, Charley," Gary attempted to soothe her, but she shrugged away from his comforting touch.

"How could I be such a fool?" She bounded

to her feet and began pacing the living room. She switched from cursing Shad to berating herself. "I should have had more sense than to fall in love with him. I must have been crazy."

"You aren't the first person to make that discovery," Gary advised and studied her worriedly. Her lightning changes of mood left him confused and uncertain how to react.

"He told me—he warned me that he'd be moving on, but I thought—" She stopped, closing her mouth at the knife-sharp surge of pain. When she continued there was a betraying quiver to her voice. "I thought he'd love me so much he'd change his mind."

"You'll get over him, Charley—in time," he comforted.

She turned on him in a blaze of anger. "No, I won't! I won't get over him—not ever! I'll never stop loving him—not even when I die! I'll come back and I'll haunt him!" she declared.

"You don't know what you're saying." He looked at her uneasily.

"Yes, I do," Charley insisted and spun away. The beginnings of a sob started again and she pressed the balled handkerchief against her mouth and sniffed in a breath. Her eyes were watering again, blurring her vision. "Do you think he'll come back, Gary?" The question was barely above a whisper. When he didn't answer, she pivoted around to face him and repeated it. "Do you?"

He tried to squarely meet her gaze and failed. "I don't know." He evaded the question with an indefinite answer.

"But you must have an opinion," Charley insisted. "Do you think he'll come back? Not right away, maybe, but someday?"

Her brother clasped his hands together and studied them, taking his time before answering her. Finally he lifted his head and shook it sadly. "I don't think he'll come back, Charley. Shad couldn't have made it any plainer that he wanted to leave."

She swallowed in a breath, feeling the last hope die with Gary's answer. She looked away, blinking at the hot tears scalding her eyes. "I would have gone with him if he'd asked me," she said hoarsely. "I would have lived out of the back end of that truck. It wouldn't have mattered—just so long as I could be with him." Even as she made the statement, she recognized that later on it might not have been enough. "But he never asked me, Gary. Not once."

"Maybe that's best," he suggested tentatively.

"The best thing would have been if I had

149

never hired him in the first place," she retorted. "I knew the moment I saw him that he was just passing through. I should have told him to keep traveling. I guess that's what he did," Charley said with a bitter laugh choked with pain. "The only problem is he walked all over my heart as he was leaving. All I can say is 'good riddance!'"

"That's right," Gary was quick to agree. "You're better off without him. He isn't the kind to ever settle down. He'd always be wandering off someplace. A leopard can't change his spots."

"I don't want a leopard. I want Shad." She switched sides again. "If he was going to leave, why didn't he go before I fell in love with him? Why did he stay so long? He said he didn't want to hurt me. For someone who didn't want to, he certainly did a bang-up job!"

"You're just torturing yourself with all this talk, Charley." Gary used the cane to push himself to his feet. "Why don't you let me fix you some coffee? You need something to settle your nerves."

A truck drove into the ranch yard. When Charley heard it she pivoted toward the door, her heart leaping into her throat. She glanced wildly at her brother. She felt dizzy with hope.

"Do you think it's Shad?" she whispered. "Maybe he's come back! Maybe he's changed his mind and finally realizes how much he cares."

Outside the engine died and a metal door was slammed shut. Charley rushed toward the front door, her feet hardly touching the floor. When she saw the man walking toward the porch, the world came crashing down around her. She sagged against the doorframe, her spirit broken by abject disappointment. She turned away and leaned her back against the wall, her eyes tightly shut.

"It's Chuck Weatherby," she informed Gary in a painful whisper, and pushed away from the wall, putting distance between herself and the front door. "I don't want to see him...or talk to him. Send him away...please."

On the far side of the room, she stopped and listened to Gary limp to the screen door. There was no creaking of the hinges so she knew he hadn't opened it to invite their neighbor inside.

"Hello, Chuck." She heard her brother greet him. "What brings you over this way?"

"Afternoon, Gary." The greeting was returned as Chuck's footsteps stopped on the porch. "Your hired man stopped over to see me earlier this afternoon. He said he was leaving and wanted to know if I could loan you one of my men for a couple days. I told him I could, but I thought afterward that maybe I ought to check with you.''

''That's good of you, Chuck,'' Gary said. ''Russell did leave and, uh, we could use an extra hand around the place for a few more days.''

Listening to Chuck's steady voice started Charley to thinking. She wiped away the last traces of tears on her face and took a deep breath. Taking a determined hold on her emotions, she turned toward the door and tilted her chin a fraction of an inch higher.

''Gary, why don't you invite Chuck in?'' she suggested in a loud voice.

Her brother cast a puzzled look over his shoulder. His glance seemed to demand that she make up her mind what she wanted. Shrugging at his inability to understand the female mind, he shifted to one side and pushed the screen door open.

''Come in, Chuck,'' he invited.

''Thank you.'' As the rancher entered the house he removed his hat and ran a hand through his auburn hair. ''Hello, Charley.'' He nodded respectfully toward her and smiled. ''I just came by to—''

''Yes, I heard,'' she interrupted him. ''Gary

and I appreciate your helping us out this way. We know it's difficult to spare a man at this time of year."

"You know that anytime I can help you out, all you have to do is ask," he insisted and moved slowly across the room toward her. "It's a shame that Russell just decided to up and walk out without giving you any notice. I warned you all along that he wasn't the kind of man you could depend on. I'm surprised that he stayed as long as he did."

"Yes, well...." Her voice wavered as she faltered over the words. She had to pause and sniff in a breath before she could continue. "We had been hoping Shad would stay longer."

His gaze narrowed on her face, noticing her red and swollen eyes and the stiffness of her carriage. "Is something wrong, Charley?" he questioned with a frown. "Have you been crying?"

Glancing at her brother, she attempted to change the subject. "Weren't you going to put some coffee on, Gary? You'd like a cup, wouldn't you, Chuck?" she offered with forced brightness. "I think there's some apple pie left from lunch."

"Yes, that would be fine." Despite his affirmative reply, the rancher hadn't been distracted from his initial observation.

"Then do you want me to put some coffee on?" Gary asked as if he half expected Charley to change her mind.

"Yes," she nodded and her brother started for the kitchen. "I'll dish up the pie while you fix the coffee." When she took a step to walk past Chuck, he caught her arm and stopped her. He made a closer study of her tear-washed face.

"You have been crying," he stated.

She flashed a glance after Gary but he'd already disappeared into the kitchen. With a sigh, she met Chuck's steady look. "Yes, I have," she admitted because she knew he would see through any excuse she made.

"Because that Shad fellow left," he guessed and released her arm.

Hanging her head, Charley nodded, "Yes."

For a minute there was only silence to follow her admission. Then she sensed the growing anger that filled the rancher. It seemed to flow from him in waves. It was strangely more comforting than any kind words would have been.

"I knew something like this would happen the minute I laid eyes on him," Chuck muttered savagely. "Rogues like that just naturally can't keep their hands off women."

"It's all right, Chuck." But she was deeply moved by his anger, which put all the blame on

Shad and none on herself. His loyalty was un-shakable.

He turned to her, his mouth tight. "Some-body should teach him a lesson. He deserves to be strung up by his heels for hurting you."

"It wouldn't change anything." Her eyes misted over with tears, all the hurt making itself felt afresh. It didn't matter how many rotten things were said about Shad, she still loved him.

"I passed him on the lane when I was driving in here," Chuck said. "He can't have gone far. If you want, I'll go get him and bring him back here."

"No." Pride stiffened her shoulders. "If he doesn't care enough to come back on his own, then I don't want him. I don't want any man that I have to drag to the altar."

Her reply stole his sense of outrage on her behalf. He breathed in deeply, his expression turning sad and grim. "Charley, I don't know what to say except... I'm sorry."

"So am I." Her faint laugh was just short of a sob.

"I'd like to get my hands on that guy for five minutes," Chuck muttered under his breath. "I'd teach him a thing or two about hurting people."

Gary hobbled into the living room and

paused, glancing from one to the other and guessing at the conversation. "The coffee is done. Should I pour it?"

"Would you stay for pie and coffee, Chuck?" Charley asked, giving him the option to refuse now that he had learned how she felt about Shad.

"I'd like to have some of that pie and coffee," he said, studying her quietly, "if you're sure I'm welcome."

"I'm sure," she nodded, then deliberately adopted a cheerful smile. "You have always been a good friend, Chuck, a very good friend. That hasn't changed."

Just a flicker of regret showed in his ruddy features before his expression was controlled to appear impassive.

"I hope you know that you can call on me whenever you need anything," he returned, not referring to his own deep affection of her. But his meaning was clear.

Charley didn't reply to that. Instead she glanced at Gary. "Let's all go into the kitchen."

All of them went through the motions as if this was an ordinary afternoon. While Gary poured the coffee, Charley sliced the pie into servings. Chuck started a conversation about ranchwork to ease the stilted silence.

The pie was consumed and a second cup of coffee drunk before Chuck sat back from the table. "That pie was delicious, Charlotte." He rubbed his expanding stomach.

"Would you like another slice?" she offered.

"No thanks, my supper is already spoiled," he refused. "Speaking of which, it's time I was getting back to my place." He stood up, hitching his trousers higher around his middle. "Ray will be over first thing in the morning."

As he turned to leave Charley came to a decision and stood up. "Chuck?" She waited until he glanced at her. "There's a dance next week in town. I wondered if you would like to take me."

"I—" He stared at her for a stunned instant, not quite certain he had heard her correctly. "I'd like that fine, Charley."

"Good," she said with a decisive nod. "I'll be ready around seven."

"I'll pick you up then," He was smiling as he pushed his hat onto his head and walked into the living room to the front door.

When she heard the door slam and his footsteps on the porch, Charley turned back to the table. Gary was staring at her with a dumbfounded expression. He shook his head as if trying to understand it all and rid himself of the confusion.

"Charley, are you all right?" he asked, combing his fingers through his hair. "What am I saying? You're not all right. That's obvious."

"Why?" She looked at him calmly, a calmness born of a new purpose.

"I don't understand you. You're not making sense," her brother declared. "Not an hour ago, you were crying your eyes out over Shad, shattered by a broken heart. I just heard you asking another man to take you out. What's going on?"

"I told Shad I wouldn't wait for him and I meant it," she replied.

"Oh, Charley," he moaned in dismay. "You don't know what you're doing."

"Yes I do," she insisted and started to clear the table.

"No, you don't. You're making a big mistake," he warned.

"No, I'm not." She set the stack of dishes down. "The way I see it I have two choices. I can either grow old and lonely waiting for Shad to come back, which he never will, or I can marry someone else and have a home and a family."

"You aren't serious?" Gary stared at her. "Are you saying that you are going to marry Chuck?"

"Why not?" Her hands were on her hips in mute challenge. "He's a good man, solid and dependable. You've said so. Shad even said he would make a wonderful husband for me. He couldn't have a higher recommendation than that, could he?" There was a trace of sarcasm and bitterness in her voice.

"That is no reason to marry a man." Gary shook his head at her reasoning.

"Listen, Gary—" her chin quivered slightly "—chances are I'm never going to love anybody the way I did Shad again. So I might as well marry someone I like and respect. Chuck might not win any prizes, but he is nice."

"Okay, maybe there is some logic in what you say," he conceded. "But don't rush into anything on the rebound, Charley. Don't marry him for spite. Promise me."

"I promise," she agreed.

CHAPTER EIGHT

FOR THE NEXT TWO MONTHS, Charley managed to stay busy. There was a lot of work to be done on the ranch that occupied her time even though Gary had fully recovered from his broken leg. She continued to see Chuck on her free time, more frequently than she ever had before.

On the outside she appeared cheerful and fun-loving. But it was only on the outside. She worked a lot, played a lot and laughed a lot—trying not to feel the enormous emptiness inside. Where her heart had been, there seemed to be one big hollow ache. It throbbed through her with a never ending rhythm.

She never stopped thinking about Shad or remembering. Every time a vehicle pulled into the ranch yard she held her breath, hoping even when she knew it was useless. There was even a vague expectancy when she looked through the mail but she never heard from him—not a word.

Sometimes Charley would gaze at the ragged line of the Sawtooth Mountains and wonder where he was and what he was seeing. She would close her eyes and picture him as clearly as if he was standing in front of her—his thick and vital crow-black hair, his bold blue eyes always glinting with lively interest and his lean, handsome features. A tear would slide down her cheek, leaving a hot trail to remind her the pain of losing him hadn't eased.

Charley wiped another tear from her cheek and turned away from the mirror. With a determined effort she shook away the hurt and fixed a smile on her mouth. Her shoulders were straight and square and her step was light as she walked out of her bedroom into the upstairs hall. She made it a point not to glance at the spare room to the right of the stairs, passing it to descend them.

Gary was entering the house by the front door when she emerged from the stairwell. He paused at the sight of her all dressed up, his glance warm with brotherly appreciation for the results.

"Do you like my new dress?" She did a slow

pirouette to show it off. The plum skirt flared, then swirled against her legs when she stopped. "I splurged the other day and bought it. This is the 'in' color now. Next year no one will probably be caught dead wearing it but I couldn't resist it."

"It's beautiful," he assured her.

"I thought so." Charley glanced down to check the fit and smoothed her hand over the waistline, enjoying the feel of the velour fabric. "Do you think Shad will like it?"

"Shad?" Her brother's voice came back low and sadly questioning.

Her head jerked up as she realized what she had said, her pretense shattering for an instant before she recovered.

"That was a slip of the tongue," she insisted with forced lightness. "I meant Chuck."

"It was a slip of the truth," Gary corrected.

"That's beside the point." Charley couldn't argue with him. "Do you think *Chuck* will like my new dress?"

"Yes," he agreed dryly. "Chuck is so crazy about you that if you were wearing a sackcloth he would think it was beautiful."

"This is hardly a sackcloth." She glanced at her watch. "I'd better get my coat. He'll be here shortly to pick me up."

"Where are you going?" Gary watched her walk to the coat closet.

"We're going to Twin Falls for Sunday dinner and maybe take in a matinee." She removed her suede coat with its fur collar from the hanger. "There's a salad in the refrigerator and you can grill yourself a steak."

"What time will you be home?"

"I don't know," she replied, folding the coat over her arm. "It might be late. We have a special occasion to celebrate today."

"Oh?" Gary lifted an eyebrow and frowned. "What's that?"

"It isn't every day that a girl gets herself engaged." The corners of her mouth were curved upward.

Her brother looked grim. "I suppose Chuck proposed to you again."

"No." She shook her head. "As a matter of fact he hasn't even brought up the subject of marriage these last two months. Usually he would have mentioned it a half dozen times. But if he doesn't propose to me today, then I'm going to ask him."

"Charley," he sighed. "You may be able to kid yourself but you can't kid me. Shad might be out of your sight, but he hasn't been out of your mind for a single minute."

"I won't deny that, Gary." She couldn't because it was true. Drawing a deep breath, she steadily met his gaze. "But if he hasn't missed me by now, then he never will."

"Are you being fair to Chuck?" he reasoned. "Don't you think it's wrong to marry him when you're in love with someone else?"

"No, I don't think it's wrong—not if Chuck is willing," Charley replied. "As long as we both go into marriage with our eyes wide open, we can make it."

"You can make your lives miserable, that's what you'll do," her brother insisted.

"Gary, it is *our* lives and *our* decision," she reminded him.

"Yes, and I don't like the idea of standing silently on the sidelines while you ruin it," he stated grimly. "You are rushing into something you aren't ready for, Charley. You're doing it because you've been hurt. Stop and think."

"I have. I've thought it all through very carefully. I know what I'm doing even if you don't think I do."

A car drove into the yard as Charley finished. She steadied the foolish leap of her heart. "Chuck's here," she said and walked over to kiss her brother on the cheek. "I'll be home tonight sometime."

A grim resignation kept him silent until she reached the door. "I only want you to be happy, Charley," her brother said to explain his opposition to her plans.

"I know." Her mouth twisted in a rueful smile before she pushed open the door and stepped outside to meet Chuck coming up the walk.

"Hi!" She adopted a bright lighthearted air as she paused at the top of the steps. Slipping into her coat, she breathed in the crisp autumn air. "It's going to be a beautiful day," Charley declared on a determinedly optimistic note.

The serrated peaks of the mountain range were cloaked with snow, standing out sharply against a turquoise blue sky. On the slopes the dark green of the pine forests ringed the white mountain crests. Stands of aspen groves shimmered gold in the bright sun.

"We'd better enjoy it," Chuck replied. "Winter won't be long in coming."

Charley pulled her gaze away from the mountains that had called to Shad and insisted he come see what was on the other side. As she looked at Chuck his freshly scrubbed appearance reminded her of a little boy all slicked up in his Sunday best. It was strange how Shad seemed so much more a man in her eyes when

Chuck was the older of the two. Yet Chuck looked at the mountains and resisted their beauty. His outlook was more practical. Winter was coming and Charley wanted in out of the cold.

"Are you ready?" He paused at the bottom of the steps and studied her closely when she continued to stand on the porch.

After a second's hesitation she started down the steps. "Yes, I'm ready." She reached out to take his hand. For a slim second she allowed herself to wonder if she wasn't selfishly reaching out for the comfort and warmth he offered without considering that she was depriving him of something he needed in return.

It was easy to relax in Chuck's company even though she made it a point to enjoy herself and act happier than she truly was. They had many mutual friends and mutual interests, incidents to recall and a background they shared in common. With Chuck she was comfortable. He was an old family friend, solid and reliable, someone she could respect and trust. He was also staid and unexciting, able to arouse her affection, but not her passion. But Charley refused to consider any of those things.

Chuck treated her to a big Sunday dinner, a full-course meal complete with soup, salad and entree. When Charley attempted to beg off the dessert, declaring she couldn't eat another bite, he became insistent.

"Have some ice cream," he said. "There's always room for that." When she shook her head to refuse, he glanced at the waitress. "Bring her a chocolate sundae."

"Chuck," she protested, "I'm stuffed, honestly. Besides, do you know how many calories there are in a chocolate sundae? Are you trying to fatten me up for market?"

"That is exactly what I'm doing," he admitted. He smiled at her, but the smile didn't quite reach his eyes. "You've lost weight lately. You could do with some extra pounds."

What he didn't mention was why she had lost weight, but it didn't need to be said. Both of them knew the cause—Shad. Even that veiled reference was enough to make Charley end her protest. The weight loss was one of the reasons she had bought the new dress. Most of her clothes didn't fit her properly anymore.

"All right, you've twisted my arm." She forced out a laugh and glanced at the waitress. "A chocolate sundae," she affirmed his order.

As the girl left, Chuck eyed Charley with approval. "You're finally showing some sense."

"I don't know about that," she returned. "I

167

probably won't be able to move after eating that.''

After dinner their plans to attend one of the movie matinees fell by the wayside. There was nothing playing at any of the theaters that particularly caught their interest. When Charley suggested that they walk off some of their dinner, Chuck agreed.

Hand in hand they strolled along the business district and gazed into shop windows at the merchandise displayed. They stopped now and then to look and admire and wander on.

Charley pointed at a window. ''Would you look at that? Christmas decorations!'' she exclaimed in disapproval. ''Halloween isn't even here yet. Christmas is starting earlier every year.''

''Do you mean you haven't started your Christmas shopping yet?'' Chuck teased as they continued on to the next shop.

''No. I'm one of those who waits until the last week, then runs around trying to buy everything at once.'' She smiled at herself. ''To me, that's the Christmas spirit.''

The next shop was a jewelry store. In its front window there was a display of wedding rings. Unwillingly Charley paused to look. The thought of exchanging vows with anyone but

Shad gave her a chilling attack of cold feet. But she had made her decision earlier, and she wouldn't retreat from it. The smile on her lips felt brittle when she glanced at Chuck.

"If you are interested in buying something to stuff in my Christmas stocking, one of those rings would be nice," she prompted him.

He eyed her warily, not certain whether she was serious or merely joking. In his uncertainty, he chose the latter. "I suppose that would be an example of good things coming in small packages."

"Yes, it would," she said, then realized he wasn't going to take the hint. He wasn't a man who appreciated subtleties. She had rejected him too many times in the past. This time she would have to speak plainer. Hesitating, she gathered her resolve. "You once asked me to marry you, Chuck, and I turned you down. I'd like you to ask me again."

There was a long, silent moment when she thought he was going to refuse. When he looked away, avoiding her gaze, Charley was certain of it.

"You're still in love with him, aren't you?" He stared into the jewelry-store window.

The question hurt as much as her answer. "Yes." She saw him close his eyes and knew it was painful for him to hear, too. "But that doesn't necessarily mean I can't grow to care for another man." Charley didn't try to pretend to Chuck that she loved him.

"I've never stopped loving you, Charlotte." He continued to stare into the window. "And I've never stopped hoping that you'd get over him and turn to me. But you're not over him."

There wasn't any way she could argue with that so she didn't try. "The tables have reversed, haven't they? Always before, you were the one who wanted to marry. Now it's me." She smiled at the irony of the situation and Chuck finally turned to look at her. Her smile faded into a serious expression. "I would be proud to be your wife, Chuck. And I'll be a good one, too. I'll make sure that you are never sorry you married me."

After considering her words for a minute, he reached inside his coat pocket and took out a jeweler's ring box. He held it in his hand, studying it. "I bought this for you three years ago and I've been waiting all this time to give it to you, wondering if the day would ever come when you'd accept it."

"Chuck," she whispered and felt empathy for all he'd gone through.

"Every time I've seen you, it's been in my

pocket...just in case," he added with a quirking smile, then paused to nervously clear his throat. "Will you marry me, Charley?" he proposed formally.

"Yes." Her voice wavered on the answer and she tried to pretend it wasn't caused by reluctance. It had been her decision.

His hand trembled as he opened the box and removed the ring. Her left hand felt as cold as ice when she offered it to him so he could place the ring on her finger. She flinched inwardly at the touch of the gold ring, a ring that wasn't given by Shad.

"I had to guess at the size," Chuck explained as he slipped it on. "It's loose." His glance held a silent apology.

"That's all right," Charley assured him. "It can be made smaller." As a dutiful bride-to-be she was obliged to admire the engagement ring. A cluster of small diamonds surrounded a center stone. It was a more elaborate ring than she would have chosen for herself, but she wouldn't hurt his feelings by saying so. "It's beautiful, Chuck."

"I hoped you would like it."

When she saw the way he was looking at her, she realized he expected something more in the way of a reaction than just words. She made the

initial move to kiss him and sensed his disappointment at her lukewarm response to the
pressure of his mouth. It was something she was
going to have to work on, but she was confident
that in time she would find some pleasure in his
embrace.

Drawing back, he smiled at her. "You don't
pick the best places to ask a man to propose to
you," he chided. "This happens to be a public
street, in case you haven't noticed."

If it had been Shad kissing her, she would
have been oblivious to the passing traffic. With
Chuck, she was conscious of it—as he was. She
tucked her hand inside the crook of his arm so
they would start walking again.

When she glimpsed their reflections in the
glass panes of a storefront, she thought they
made an incongruous pair. But perhaps they
didn't. They were both in love with someone
who didn't love them.

"I was thinking that maybe we could get married after the first of the year," Chuck suggested. "Things are slower on the ranch during
the winter. It would be easier for me to be away.
We could go somewhere warm for our honey-
moon. Acapulco, maybe."

For a minute she almost panicked, feeling
that she was being rushed. She steadied her

nerves and smiled a tremulous agreement. "Yes, that would be a good time."

"I'm glad you agree. I know there's probably a lot you have to do—" he began.

Charley quickly interrupted him. "I'd rather not have a big wedding. Just the family and a few close friends." She couldn't take the hypocrisy of a large church wedding with hundreds of guests. "Do you mind?"

"I don't mind," he assured her. "As a matter of fact, I wasn't looking forward to the idea of wearing a tuxedo. But I know women like all that fanciness."

"Not this woman," she corrected. "I just want a simple ceremony."

The car was parked just ahead of them. Chuck paused. "I was just thinking."

"About what?" She cast him a sideways glance.

"I know it's probably old-fashioned, but I was just thinking that maybe I should take you home so I can speak to your brother."

"I think I'm old enough that I don't need his permission," Charley smiled. "But we can go if you want."

There was a vague reluctance about facing her brother. She was having enough second thoughts of her own without learning of his misgivings. Now that the ring was on her finger and the engagement was an accomplished fact, Charley was frightened by what she had done. Her only consolation was that the alternative of being alone was more frightening.

When they returned to the ranch, they found Gary in the machine shed fixing the spare tire for his truck. He showed surprise at seeing Charley home so early.

"I didn't expect you until tonight," he commented.

"There weren't any movies playing that we wanted to see," Charley replied.

"Actually—" Chuck cleared his throat, his normally ruddy complexion turning redder "—we came back because...I asked Charley to marry me and she accepted. We wanted you to be the first to know."

His expression darkened with a thunderous frown as Gary turned his accusing glance on her. "I didn't really think you'd do it." Feeling the full weight of his disapproval, she inwardly flinched.

Chuck missed his meaning and laughed. "Neither did I. I've been asking her for so long that I couldn't believe it when she indicated she would accept." He sobered under Gary's cold glance. "Since you are the man of the family, so to speak, I thought it was only proper if I—''

"I suppose you've come to ask my permission," her brother growled.

"Yes," Chuck hesitated at Gary's attitude of angry disgust.

"Damn it, man!" Gary swore. "I knew Charley wasn't responsible for her actions, but I credited you with having more sense then to make such a fool move, Chuck."

"Stop it, Gary," Charley protested in a furious underbreath.

"I'd love to stop this ridiculous marriage before it can take place!" he snapped. "Unfortunately you don't need my permission. You're both stupid enough to go through with this thing without it!"

"I'm sorry that you disapprove," Chuck murmured.

"For God's sake, Chuck, open your eyes!" her brother insisted. "She's still in love with him. Can't you see that?"

"Yes, I know," he admitted grudgingly. "We discussed it."

"Are you prepared to live with a woman who is in love with someone else?" Gary challenged. "To sleep with her, knowing that she's imagining another man in your place."

"That is enough!" Her temper flared.

"No, it isn't enough!" he countered, matching her fire. "It has to be said. Chuck has a right to know what the hell he's letting himself in for. It's something I don't think either one of you have faced!"

"We have," Chuck asserted.

Gary glanced from one to the other, then released a long, weary breath. "I guess there isn't anything else I can say then, is there?"

"We haven't set a date yet for the wedding," Charley said. "But it will be sometime after the first of the year. I'd like you to give me away, Gary."

"You know I will." A look of resignation spread across his face. "But I still think you're making a mistake. I'm sorry."

"It's going to be a simple wedding with only a few guests, nothing elaborate." It seemed safest to discuss the wedding plans. There could be little argument about the details.

"That's a blessing," Gary murmured dryly.

"It's really your blessing we want," Charley said.

"You have my blessing," he sighed heavily. "I wish you both all the happiness in the world. But that doesn't change the fact that I don't believe you're going to find it together."

"We thank you for your wishes," Chuck put his arm around her to show that it came from both of them.

"Don't thank me." Gary shook his head. "I probably should be trying to pound some sense into your heads."

"I'd like to have an informal get-together here next weekend and invite some of our friends so Chuck and I can announce our engagement," Charley explained. "Is that all right with you? It is your house."

"It's your home, too," Gary replied. "You can have all the parties you want. I doubt if I'll feel like celebrating. Excuse me—" he brushed past them "—I'm going to the house and wash up."

When he had gone, Charley murmured, "I'm sorry, Chuck."

"He made it pretty plain what he thought of our chances, didn't he?" he sighed.

"Don't pay any attention to him," she insisted.

"That isn't easy."

"Will you stay for supper?" she invited, not wanting him to leave in this mood.

"No, thanks; I'd better be getting back home." He kissed her cheek before he removed his arm from around her shoulders. He took a step away, then paused. "Do you know that I always knew this would be the happiest day of my life? It's strange because I don't feel happy. Not at all."

"It'll be all right," she whispered, trying to convince herself as much as him, but Chuck hadn't heard her as he walked away.

CHAPTER NINE

ALTOGETHER eight couples attended the engagement party in addition to Gary, Chuck and herself. Charley had brought the chairs in from the kitchen so there would be a place for everyone to sit in the living room, but most of them were standing and talking. The kitchen table was being used as a buffet table, holding the refreshments—an assortment of chips, sandwiches and cheeses. A variety of soft drinks provided setups and Chuck had furnished a case of beer.

On the surface the party appeared to be a success, but it was proving to be more of an ordeal than Charley had expected. She and Chuck had been dating for years, yet everyone seemed amazed by their engagement. Every time she turned around, surprise was being voiced by one of their friends.

This time it was Betty Todd. "I just can't get over it!" she declared in a voice that always seemed one degree too loud. "I never dreamed you two would actually become engaged."

"As you can see, that's exactly what we've done," Charley assured her with a stiff smile.

"Let me look at your ring." She grabbed Charley's hand and turned and twisted it to watch the flash of light from the diamonds. "It must have cost Chuck a fortune. Did he say how much he had to pay for it?"

"No. And I didn't ask him. I didn't think it was any of my business." *And it certainly isn't any of yours,* she thought to add, but manners forbade it.

"You should get it insured, Charley," Betty advised her. "It's so loose. Why, what would happen if it slipped off and you lost it?"

"We are having it made smaller so that won't happen," she explained with waning patience. "Chuck is taking it into the jeweler's next week."

"You and Chuck." Her friend returned to the same theme. "Isn't it something after all this time?" she marveled.

"I don't see why it's such a surprise to everyone," Charley declared at last.

"You've been going together for years and lately—" Betty paused to shrug "—there have been rumors flying around that you were having an affair with that hired man you had working here."

Charley blanched. A hand touched her shoulder and she turned with a start.

"Hi, sis," Gary said, a smile masking the alertness of his gaze as it traveled over her pale face. Then he shifted his attention to the other woman. "Hi, Betty. I think Glenda wanted to talk to you. She's over there with Sue and the others." He gestured toward a group of women.

"I'd better see what she wants. Excuse me."

As the woman crossed the room Charley sipped at the glass of fruit punch in her hand. "Your timing was excellent, Gary."

"I thought you looked like you needed rescuing," he murmured in an aside. "Where's Chuck? I thought he'd be with you."

"He's right over there, talking to Clyde Barrows." She nodded to the trio of men only a few feet from her. "We aren't a pair of giggling teenagers who are inseparable."

"I know. That's what worries me," her brother replied dryly.

"Please, Gary, don't start in on that," Charley protested in a taut weary tone.

"Sorry. This is a party, isn't it? How's your drink? Would you like another?" he offered.

"No," she refused even though the ice cubes had melted and turned the drink watery.

The front door opened and closed, letting a draft of cool night air into the room. Thinking one of the guests had stepped out for some fresh air, Charley absently glanced toward the door. She looked straight into a pair of glittering blue eyes. Shock riveted her to the floor.

She was hallucinating. Her mind was playing cruel tricks on her. It couldn't be Shad.

Yet he was crossing the room, walking directly toward her. Dressed in a white shirt and black-quilted vest, he appeared too solid and real to be a mirage. Joy soared through her at the sight of him, lifting her to the unscalable heights of heaven. Her shining gaze wandered over the heavy blackness of his hair and his handsome masculine features, so tanned and vigorous. When he stopped in front of her, it was his eyes that captivated her. The smoldering intensity of their blue light was breathtaking.

"Hello, Charley, my darling." The lazy drawl of his low voice was a caress, touching her and assuring her of his existence.

"Shad," she whispered his name.

His glance impatiently swept the gathering of people only just beginning to notice his presence. "It looks like I'm crashing somebody's party. What is it? A birthday celebration?" His glance returned to Charley. His question brought her sharply back to reality and she had to lower her gaze. Shad looked beyond her. "Is it yours, Gary?"

"No, it isn't my birthday," her brother replied dryly and left the explanation to Charley.

"You're certainly looking fit since the last time I saw you. How is the leg?" Shad made the polite inquiry of her brother but a hard edge began to underscore his voice.

"Good as new." Gary kept his responses short and to the point, inviting no further discussion of the subject.

"Is this all the welcome I get, Charley?" Shad's voice came back to her, low and demanding, rough with frustration. "I know I hurt you when I left but— Aren't you glad to see me?"

Tears were in her eyes when she lifted her gaze. All the bitterness and agony of these past two months were written in their pain-filled depths. There was frustration, too, that Shad should return just when she had reconciled herself to never seeing him again—when she had promised herself to Chuck and taken his ring.

"Why did you wait so long to come?" she accused in a hoarse whisper, her throat raw and throbbing painfully with awful despair.

"Because I was stupid and blind." His look became warmly possessive as he brought his hands up to grip her shoulders.

The touch of him opened a wound so deeply painful that she started trembling. She loved him so much that it became a physical hurt. The numbing misery of the past two months was gone and every raw nerve in her body became sensitive to him. She ached to be held in his arms and feel the healing beauty of his kisses, but she was kept from seeking his embrace by the diamond ring burning the flesh of her finger. Charley clutched her drink glass with both hands to keep from returning his touch.

"It took me a while to realize it was your voice I heard whispering in the breeze, calling to me," Shad murmured. "You were the shining warmth I felt when I walked in the sunlight. There was nothing over the next hill that was better than what I'd left behind. The best thing in my life had already happened to me and that was you. Anything else would only be hollow echoes of what I'd known. I was surrounded by emptiness, Charley, and the bittersweet memories of you.''

''Oh, Shad.'' She closed her eyes tightly, but the tears squeezed through her lashes to run down her cheeks.

''You have every right to be angry and call me a thousand kinds of fool,'' he admitted. ''You told me how it would be before I left, and you were right. I can't live without you, Charley. You are my life.''

Opening her eyes, she blinked through the wall of tears to see the absolute certainty of his ardent expression, the searing fire of his blue gaze. There was a movement beside her. She half turned and recognized Chuck's blurred form.

''Shad, this isn't a birthday party.'' Her voice was husky with the pain of her announcement. ''We are celebrating my engagement to Chuck. We're going to be married.''

She felt the stillness that rocked him and drained the color from his face, leaving him white beneath his tan. His surprise was so total that she felt the surge of anger. She hadn't heard a single word from him in all this time. Yet Shad had come back, fully expecting her to forgive and forget all that she had suffered because of him. Just for a second, she hated his male ego and wanted to hurt him as she had been hurt—deep and wounding.

"I told you I wouldn't wait!" she lashed out with sobbing fury.

A violent shudder racked his lean frame as his hands fell from her shoulders and he turned his head away. He appeared to brace himself to absorb the aftershock of the blow. When he turned back to her, his eyes were dark and haunted. The desolation she saw almost made Charley cry out, but Chuck touched her arm and took the glass from her trembling hands before she dropped it. The movement pulled Shad's gaze to Chuck.

"Congratulations." His voice sounded choked as his large hand reached out to shake Chuck's. "I think you know you're a lucky man to have a woman like Charley."

"Yes, I think I do." Chuck sounded gruff and defensive.

His tortured gaze slid back to her. "I guess I deserve this," Shad said in a low murmur. Her throat muscles were so tightly constricted that Charley couldn't speak. She could only look at him in mute agony. "He will be a better husband for you than I could ever be. I told you before that I thought he was a good man for you."

"Yes." She remembered it too well. Shad had advised her to marry him.

He didn't take his darkly haunted eyes from her face, but he addressed his next request to Chuck. "Do you have any objections if I kiss your fiancée? Just one last time."

The praise from Shad must have assured Chuck that there was no threat, because he gave his permission. "I have no objections."

Shad stepped forward and cupped her face in his hands, his thumbs lightly stroking her cheeks. A moan came from her throat, so soft that it was barely audible; a tiny cry of utter longing. He brought his face closer to hers, his gaze seeming to memorize every feature.

"No one will ever love you as much as I do, Charley." His low drawl was so quiet only she could hear what he was saying. "I don't have to travel over the next hill to know that. It probably doesn't mean anything to you but I'm not drifting anymore. I've crossed my last river."

Her breath came in a sharp gasp, then his lips were trembling against hers, moving over them softly. She swayed against him, her hands spreading across his smooth vest. A raw hunger claimed him, hardening the kiss with its fierce urgency. Charley responded to its demands, aware only of her deep, abiding love for him.

187

Then Shad was breaking it off, letting her go abruptly to turn away. He muttered an emotionally thick, "Take care of her," to Chuck and left a dazed Charley standing there to watch him stride across the room and out the front door.

"Are you going to let him walk away?" It was Gary who prodded her into awareness.

"What else can I do?" She turned her tear-filled eyes onto her brother.

"You love him, Charley. Damn it, go after him," he declared impatiently. "Don't stand here crying!"

"Was this your idea?" she demanded, remembering how determined her brother had been to put a stop to her marriage to Chuck. "Did you ask Shad to come here tonight? Did you do this?"

"If I had known how to get a hold of him or where to find him, I would have dragged him here, willing or not," Gary admitted. "But I didn't. He came back to you on his own. That has to prove something to you. Are you going to let him leave?"

Her gaze rushed to the front door where Shad had gone. She longed to run after him but she hesitated, twisting the diamond on her finger. She looked at it, trying not to feel the weight of her promise to Chuck, a man so unswerving in his loyalty.

"You want to go to him, don't you?" His sad voice spoke to her.

"Chuck." She turned to him, an aching regret sweeping through her at the defeat in his expression. "I don't want to hurt you."

"I guess I always knew it wasn't meant to be for us. I've just been kidding myself, pretending that you might care for me someday." His mouth twisted in a rueful line as he bent his head.

"I'm sorry," she said, and meant it.

He was shaking a little as he took her left hand. "I put this ring on your finger and I'll take it off." It slipped off easily at his touch. "You're free, Charley. Go to him. He's the one you want."

Charley wanted to thank him, but Gary was already pushing her toward the door. "Hurry up before he leaves."

She started out at a walk. Before she had taken three steps, she was running. Distantly she heard the astonished murmur of voices from the guests, but she was past caring what anybody thought as she raced out the door and into the night.

At the top of the porch steps she paused to

search the shadowed yard of parked vehicles for Shad. There was a second of panic until she noticed a dejected figure leaning against the cab of a pickup, an arm hooked over a side mirror for support. She flew down the steps and through the shadows toward him.

"Shad!"

He stiffened at the sound of her voice and turned to face her, his posture rigid. She stopped short of him, able to make out his lean features and the pain carved in them. Love kindled a fire that sent its warm glow through her body.

"I don't know where you think you are going, Shad Russell." She was smiling as she wiped away the moisture on her cheeks. "But this time, you aren't leaving without me."

"Charley." He took a step forward and stopped.

She guessed the cause for his hesitancy and explained, "Chuck has the ring. The engagement is off. You are the only man I love—the only man I have ever loved."

With a shout of delight Shad swept her into his arms, lifting her into the air and whirling her around. She was laughing with free-flowing happiness when he finally stopped. For a breathless moment they both looked at each other.

When his mouth settled onto hers, his kiss wiped out all the pain and torment. Now there was room only for the boundless joy they found in each other. Their appetite was insatiable, one that not even time could reduce.

Ending the kiss, Shad kept his arm around her as he opened the driver's door of the truck and gave her a push. "Inside," he ordered.

"Where are we going?" Not that it mattered as long as they were together.

"We're going across the state line into Nevada and find ourselves the first preacher who will marry us," he stated as he climbed behind the wheel once she was in the cab.

"If that's a proposal, I accept." Charley laughed.

Reaching in the side pocket of his vest, he took out a small box and dropped it into her lap as he started the engine. "There is even a ring to go with the proposal."

She opened it and drew a breath of delight. It was a simple diamond solitaire set in a wide band of gold. "It's perfect; it's beautiful. I love it." Her arms went around his neck as she placed an appreciative kiss on the corner of his mouth.

"Careful, I'm driving," he warned mockingly, and kissed her lightly on the lips before negotiating the truck through the parked cars. "Aren't you interested in where we're going after we're married?"

"Where?" If it was to the ends of the earth, she'd follow him.

"To my ranch near the Bitterroots. I've spent the past two weeks fixing the house and modernizing the kitchen for you. New draperies, the works," he said. "If there is anything you don't like, you can change it."

"We're going to have a home?"

"I told you. I've crossed my last river." He stopped the truck to take her in his arms and drown in her love.